SURRENDERED
ON THE
FRONTIER

JANE HENRY

Published by Stormy Night Publications and Design, LLC.
www.StormyNightPublications.com

Cover design by Korey Mae Johnson
www.koreymaejohnson.com

Images by The Killion Group and 123RF/Vadav Volrab

1st Print Edition. September 2016

ISBN-13: 978-1539145080

ISBN-10: 1539145085

FOR AUDIENCES 18+ ONLY

CHAPTER ONE: A MEMORABLE ENCOUNTER

My heart thundered in my chest, my eyes still adjusting to the darkness of the bedroom as I woke with a start. Wiping a hand across my brow, I sat up, thankful the details of my dream were fading already. I'd worked hard to bury those memories.

When our house had burnt to the ground, set ablaze by my husband's own hands, and he had been shot to death a short time later, we were taken in by the Stanley family. Ma, the matriarch of the brood, lived with her sons Matthew and Samuel. Matthew, at twelve years old, was just four years older than my eight-year-old Hannah. I was only twenty-three years old, and Samuel three years my senior.

The townsfolk had done a regular house-raising for us, and now we were the proud owners of a brand new home. There was a small window in my room—a rarity in the cabins on the plains, but Samuel, my neighbor and friend, had insisted I have one when our new home was built.

"Flowers need light to grow," he'd said. And so the men raising our house had put in a window. I'd heard Geraldine, Samuel's sister-in-law, grumble that she didn't have a window in her bedroom, and my friend Pearl had told her

1

to hush. Now, as I lay in bed, I saw the faintest trace of morning light peeking through the window that Samuel had given me. It was just before daybreak.

I tiptoed to the front room after dressing. Hannah didn't need to wake for another hour, and she was a good girl. She'd get up and get ready for school and do her chores. We'd breakfast together, and I'd go about my day. But first, I needed to fetch water. I liked the early morning quiet.

I hummed quietly to myself, walking along the path that led to the woods, but ceased humming as the creek drew near. I didn't want to miss the low coo of the mourning dove, a familiar sound that brought me comfort. In the distance came the telltale banging of a woodpecker and the soft twitter of a songbird.

"Ain't right for a woman to be out about these parts alone."

I nearly jumped out of my skin at the voice behind me. My bucket clattered to the ground.

"Land's sake, you don't have to scare me out of my wits," I muttered, though my cheeks flushed slightly. Samuel's serious, cornflower blue eyes peeked at me from beneath his wide-brimmed hat, his lightly bearded jaw clenched as he stood behind me with his arms folded across his chest.

My heart still danced in my chest, and the fright made me angry. As he picked up my bucket, I swiped a hand at him, trying to snatch it back. His hand shot out and he grasped my wrist just before my hand brushed his. His brows lifted ever so slightly and he shook his head at me with a frown.

"Now, little Ruth, you be a good girl," he chided, his voice dropping an octave. "There's no need for you to be losin' your temper."

"I'm not a *girl*, Samuel," I said haughtily. "I'm a woman, one who's been fetching her water by the creek alone for years. Now hand me my bucket."

"You didn't fetch water by the creek when you lived with

me."

"Only because you wouldn't let me, but you can't stop me now."

Another small shake of his head. "Is that right?"

"Give me my bucket!" I said, anger rising.

His frown deepened. "Say please."

Oh, the audacity! I fumed and tried to pull my wrist away from him, but he held fast.

"It's mine, now *give* it to me."

His brows rose further. He was implacable. "I won't give it to you until you say please."

"Confound you! *Please!*" He released me and handed me my bucket, though he pursed his lips and his jaw tightened.

"Woman, why on earth are you goin' to the creek, when you could just go get your water from the well?"

I felt a bit embarrassed at that point, and looked away. "I like the walk," I said. "Sometimes by the creek in the early morning, I can hear the call of the sparrow, or the mourning dove. And sometimes I see the white-tailed deer." I turned and faced him bravely, which took a bit of gumption, considering he was staring at me steadily and dwarfed me in size. I was the 'runt of the litter,' my ma liked to say, shorter than any other woman I'd known, and certainly just a wisp of a thing next to the tall, sturdy Samuel. "I like being alone, and I've not been hurt yet. Anyway, if anything tried to hurt me, I'm fast and run like the wind."

He took a step toward me and put a finger to the wisp of hair that had escaped from the hasty knot at my nape, tucking it behind my ear.

"Is that right?" he asked, but it was more a statement than a question, a low murmur. I looked down shyly. I'd known Samuel now for over a year, and as of late, things seemed to be a bit different. He felt less of a friend and now more... something else. I felt quieter, and my anger began to diminish.

His voice dropped lower. "Do you want me to leave, then, Ruth?"

"Well, no," I said slowly.

"Good," he said, and his eyes were smiling. "Because I ain't goin' away." He sobered as he stepped closer to me. "I won't be allowin' you to go to the creek alone now."

"It's not your place to allow or disallow," I said.

He smiled softly at that, but his eyes grew serious. "While I'm standing here, it is."

Anger flared in my chest and I wanted to smack him again. "And what will you to do stop me?" I asked, glaring.

"I'll take you right up off that ground and toss you over my shoulder," he said, and a muscle twitched in his jaw. His eyes flashed. "And if I had to? March you back to the barn and tie you to a post so you don't get away."

Something about the way he suggested overpowering me set my heart to stuttering again. "I'm not afraid of you and your highhanded ways," I hissed.

He leaned in closer, his voice deep and low as he spoke. "Well, maybe you *ought* to be. I hear tell around town there's been a few women roughed up by some men travelin' in packs. Comin' in tradin' furs and movin' on, leavin' destruction in their wake. You're a tiny little thing and I could pick you right up and put you in my pocket."

Was it worth fighting him? I stepped back and sighed. "All right, then. I won't go alone." *Today,* I added internally. "Will you at least come with me, then?"

He shook his head. "No, Ruth. You have a well that's just as good, and there's no need to venture into the woods. There are rattlers, and wolves, and savages." His voice sharpened. "Use your head, woman. Come with me, now." He reached for my hand. It was the first time he'd ever taken my hand before. His hand was larger, and callused, and my own hand felt soft and small compared to his. He tugged me a bit, turning me away from the creek and back toward home. I didn't much like that he'd fancied it proper for him to tell me what to do. He wasn't my husband, my father, or my brother, and I did not owe him my obedience.

Why, then, did I feel a sort of quiet in his sturdy

presence, as I walked by his side?

"You need help around the farm today?" he asked.

"We're fine." I trotted quickly to keep up with his long strides.

"I noticed the other day your barn door is not as secure as it ought to be. I can stop on by after supper and fix that."

I was still annoyed he was being so bossy, so I tried to yank my hand away from his. He wouldn't let go. "I said I'm *fine*, Samuel, thank you. I do not need a hand."

He glanced at me sideways and scowled. "Young lady, you may not need a hand on the farm, but you could use a hand across your backside," he said in a low drawl.

I finally managed to yank my hand away from him, spinning around to glare at him. My eyes roved over him. He was much taller than I was, and his sleeves were rolled up, revealing tanned, muscled arms. His sandy brown hair was long enough to peek out from beneath his hat. Hands anchored on sturdy hips, he stood, bracing himself in front of me, two feet planted solidly. He frowned. "Are we goin' to stand here all day arguin' about where to fetch water?"

It was then that I was struck with the absurdity of the situation. My anger began to fade, and I cursed my hot temper that flared so easily. He'd made me come along with him so that I wasn't in harm's way, and told me I needed a spanking. Truth be told, I *was* acting like a spoiled child. I was suddenly repentant.

"I'm sorry," I murmured, closing my eyes. I inhaled, lifting my eyes back to his and speaking quietly. He was still frowning at me with his hands on his hips, as if to wait and see what I would do next. "Samuel, you don't deserve to be treated this way. Out here, you're one of my only friends." My voice caught. He'd been so good to me the past year, had done more work around my homestead as we prepared to move than my own husband had done in the past eight years. "Please forgive me?"

His eyes softened a bit as he nodded and took my hand again, tugging me along so we were walking back to my cabin.

"It's all right now, honey," he said. "But you're right tied up tighter than a newly strung banjo. What's eatin' you?"

"Oh, nothing. Well, nothing big, I guess."

He led us over to the well and reached for the handle, lifting up a bucket of the cool, clear water, as I held my bucket for him.

"Hannah needs new shoes, as her toes are nearly clean out of the ones she has. School's out soon, and she and I have much to do around here. I've got nothing to really fall back on, and we haven't had fresh meat in weeks. I hate hunting. Can't bear to do it. I do dearly love to eat meat. But I can't bring myself to actually fetch it. Small little things troubling me that I'll deal with."

I watched as he filled the bucket with water, and when he was done, I reached to take it. He merely shook his head.

"I can carry the bucket," I said. "I do it every day."

"Not while I'm around you don't," he muttered, reaching for my hand again, holding the bucket of water in the other hand. I allowed him to take it, and trotted beside him as we made our way back to my home. With my husband, things had been quite different. He'd not been kind and protective, like Samuel, but malicious and selfish. I wanted to purge every memory of my husband, the way he'd touched me and taken me and abused me, scorch the memories from my mind and heart. I hated every memory of him. I needed to reclaim the woman I once was.

There was only one good thing he'd ever given me, and she was waiting for me in the cabin.

"You get on with your chores, and I'll get on with mine," Samuel said as we approached the front door.

"Will you come in for some breakfast?" I asked.

He shook his head. "I'd like to, but I've got to get back. We're getting' on with the shearin' today. Aaron and Phillip are comin' to give me a hand, and then I'll be headin' on over to their places to help them." There were four Stanley brothers. Aaron was the eldest, and he was married to Pearl, who was a friend of mine. Phillip came next. He was Geraldine's husband and they'd just had their first little baby. I didn't see much of them. Samuel was next in line, and at the very end came Hannah's friend Matthew, the youngest.

"You need help with the shearing?" I asked. Often, the sheep would respond well to the gentler touch and softer voice of a woman.

"Thank you, no," Samuel said. "You've got your own work to do here. But I'll be by right soon to visit again. Noon?"

I nodded. He looked me over then, and his eyes warmed. To my surprise, he reached his hand out and it wrapped around the back of my neck. He tugged, drawing me closer to him. His mouth dipped to my forehead and he gave me a brief, chaste kiss. "You be a good girl, now, Ruth, and take care of yourself."

"I will," I said with a smile. I stood in front of the door, watching until I couldn't see him anymore. And even as I felt the warmth of his lips still upon my skin, I felt suddenly very, very alone.

• • • • • • •

Hannah sat at the table, swinging her little feet in front of her. Her hair was lighter than mine, a caramel-colored brown, neatly braided. Her freckled face was scrubbed clean, her blue eyes bright and cheerful. I marveled at the transformation my little girl had undergone in the year with just me and the Stanleys watching over her. She no longer cowered, or hid in her room in fear. She walked taller now. I was proud of my strong little girl.

We were getting used to our new home. It was still built upon the plot of land Leroy and I had staked when we were newlyweds, so fortunately I hadn't had to begin new with crops. They'd been planted in previous years, and though not maintained most recently, I'd been putting in tireless hours weeding and pruning in preparation for spring. But it was difficult for me to keep up the farm. The house and barn were sturdily built, but needed constant attention. Our livestock was meager, but also needed care.

So as Hannah chattered on and on about the book she read for school, and the new trail to the creek she and Matthew found, my mind was occupied.

How would I get what we needed? What services did I possibly have to offer? I had no idea how I could earn some extra income.

"Ma, you seem as if you're a mile away today," Hannah said, taking a long sip of milk from her tin cup.

"Oh, just much on my mind, darlin'," I said, stirring the coffee as I prepared it. The warm, pungent scent filled the room, and I smiled softly to myself. The first cup of coffee with just a bit of the fresh milk would do me good. "You need new shoes. We need supplies around here, and I need to be prepared to tend to the animals."

Hannah nodded. "Ma?"

"Yes?"

"Can I go to Mary Ellen's? She's having a birthday celebration, and I wanted to go."

I turned my back to her and faced the stove. Frowning as I poured the steaming coffee into my mug, I kept my back purposefully to Hannah, so she wouldn't see my face. I did not want her to go. It had only been a year since we had broken free from the tyranny of my husband. I wanted to shield her from all that was evil and wicked and hurtful in the world. As long as I lived, I'd never forget the way he'd raised his hands to her. I'd defended her every time, to my own detriment, and couldn't bear the thought of another soul harming her.

"I don't know," I said. I didn't want to tell her no. "I'll think on it, and let you know."

Behind me, she responded, "Yes, Ma."

I decided to change the subject. "I saw a nest full of eggs this morning when I went to get the water," I said. "And one of them is cracking open! We'll hear the chirps of baby songbirds any minute now."

My proclamation had the desired effect. Hannah's eyes shone. "Ooooh! I want to see!" she said, but I pointed to her breakfast and reminded her to finish. She quickly downed the remainder of her food, and as soon as she was done, the two of us scurried out of the house to where the nest lay in the eaves of the barn. We crept along quietly. I reveled in my daughter's shining eyes as we came upon the nest. "Three of them, Mama!" she whispered, pointing a little finger at the trio of downy little baby birds chirping and mewing for their mama. As we watched, stock still, the mama bird came flying in with a large, wiggly worm in its beak.

Hannah gasped. "Oooh, oh, the mama's gonna feed the worm to the babies!" she hissed.

"Well, of course," I said. "Birds don't nurse their young like the cows and horses."

"I know! It's just... *awful!*" she said, giving a muffled shriek as one little bird began eagerly nipping at the worm. "Oh, that little one didn't get anything to eat, because the other ones were all greedy! I wonder what it would be like to share something like that with your brothers and sisters."

"Well, now, I'm sure that mama is capable of finding more worms," I said with a chuckle.

"I can find some, too! I'll pile them all up right next to the nest where she can find them."

"Oh, that's a noble idea," I said. "But now it's time you get yourself to school."

We both started as we heard a shout right outside the barn.

"Hannah!"

"Oh, that'd be Matthew," she said, scrambling up to go meet him outside. I brushed the hay from my apron and followed behind her, the sun momentarily blinding me.

Matthew stood with his lunch pail in one hand and books in the other, his wild hair wet and slicked down, and

I remembered well the mornings he'd fight his ma, when Samuel wasn't there, until she bested him and straightened his hair out for school. If Samuel was there he'd merely give him that 'look' and say in his low voice, "Matthew, mind your ma," and Matthew would meekly comply.

As my eyes adjusted to the light, I looked with surprise to see that Samuel stood next to him. I hadn't expected Samuel to return so soon. I nodded to him, and he tipped his hat.

"All right, then, you two behave yourselves, and come straight back here for some cookies after school," I said, knowing that they'd come straight home with the promise of such a treat.

I waved as I saw them off, pleased Hannah had Matthew to watch out for her. I stood, my arms wrapped around me, enjoying the warmth of the sun. Though Samuel stood beside me, my mind was churning over all I had to do that day, so I didn't speak for a moment. I had so very much on my mind that when I heard the squall of the barn cat, I just about jumped out of my skin.

There was chirping and squawks, and sounds of a struggle just inside the barn. I gasped, thankful in the split second it took me to realize what was happening, that Hannah had already gone to school. I bolted to the barn, but Samuel got there first.

• • • • • • •

There were feathers and blood, and a proud-looking tabby cat standing with the mama bird limp in its mouth. We called the cat Cornhusk, and she was Hannah's least favorite, scrawny and aloof, but I liked her because she hunted mice with a vengeance. Cornhusk came to me and dropped the bird as an offering at my feet. I shook with fury.

"You wicked, evil thing!" I shrieked, swatting at it fiercely with my hand. It scurried away, narrowly missing my hand, and likely confused as to why I hadn't been grateful for the gift.

I fell to my knees and gently lifted the lifeless bird. Dropping the bird, I lifted my apron to my face. As tears welled in my eyes and sadness filled my chest, Samuel spoke.

"Now, Ruth, don't despair," he said. "Come here, woman, and look."

I dropped my apron.

"Every one of 'em unharmed," he murmured, picking up one of the wee baby birds in his large hand. The baby bird pecked at his palm, causing him to chuckle as he stroked one large, rough finger over the downy feathers.

"They're all safe?" I whispered.

He smiled and nodded. "They'll need some attention, of course," he said. "I mean, without their mama they won't be able to survive."

Something about watching his big, gentle hand holding the tiny baby bird made my heart twist.

"They'll need shelter, water, and food," he continued. "You can't keep 'em in here like this. Any manner of beast would get 'em. You've got a place inside?"

"Of course I do," I said. And with his help, we moved the little nest and the three baby birds into our cabin. One of the people who'd helped raise our house had fashioned a bit of a table out of a tree stump for Hannah, which stood right next to her bed and beneath the window in her room. It worked as the perfect sunny spot. The little birds chirped and squawked. I smiled as I turned to Samuel.

"What brings you here?" I asked. "I thought you were shearing the sheep today."

"Ma asked if I'd come and fetch you," he said. "Said she wanted to have your hand in helpin'. Matthew found himself a honey tree, and she said come and help, and take what you'd like."

"Honey?" I asked, as gleeful as a small child. I loved honey on my biscuits, or in my tea, and I still made a honey cake my own ma taught me to make when I was a little girl. But honey wasn't something easily found, or even easy to come by. When we did find it, we found it aplenty, and stored it away as best we could. It was liquid gold to me.

Samuel's eyes twinkled. "I think she'd much appreciate it if you'd give a hand with the dinner. You know I like your food better'n anyone else's, anyway."

I wondered for a moment if this was his polite way of saying, "Ma wants to make sure you and Hannah have enough to eat." I was quite a hand at cooking, though, and Ma said I could make a meal fit for a king with nothing more than greens from the garden and a little bit of sunshine.

When I didn't answer right away, Samuel's eyes hardened a bit. "I know that look, woman," he said.

"What look?" I responded, pretending to ignore him as I turned my back to him and tended to the little birds in my nest.

"That stubborn look that says your pride is gettin' in the way of good sense is what. When's the last time you and Hannah had meat?"

I frowned, giving him a quick glance over my shoulder. "We do just fine, thank you. Honestly, Samuel, I don't know if I have time to go with you today. I've much to do around here."

He crossed his arms on his chest and looked at me sternly. "Tell me."

"Tell you what?" I asked, feeling my irritation rising.

"What you've got to do today."

The nerve of the man! "Do you doubt my honesty?" I asked, spinning around to face him. "Or is it that you have no use for woman's work? You think that the work in the house isn't as important as the work in the field? You'd do well to remember that I have both the work of a man *and* woman on this farm!" I'd marched over to him as I spoke, so close to him now my angry exhale ruffled his shirt.

His eyes darkened. "Woman, if you hadn't been mistreated at the hand of that lowlife husband of yours, do you have any idea what I'd do to you?"

My anger flared into flames of fury. "How *dare* you

threaten me? You'd take a hand to me like he did? You wouldn't!"

He took a step toward me then—the only step between us—so that now he towered over me and I had to crane my neck to look up at his furious face.

His voice was a low, hissed whisper. "Not like he did. You insult me to even hint at such a thing. But there's a world of difference between his fist and my palm across your backside. Ruth Watson, though you try my patience, I won't spank you. But as God is my witness, if you don't close your mouth, I'll close it in the only way I can."

My stomach clenched. I knew I was acting in anger and I knew Samuel was a good man, but I was not immune to the threat of a spanking. I also didn't know how he meant to close my mouth.

I poked a finger at his chest, though I trembled. I was furious at his ridiculous statement but angrier still at my body that would betray me. For I was somehow set to flames with his warning of a spanking, my belly tingling.

"Don't you *ever*," I began, but his large hand wrapped around my smaller one, interrupting my punctuated set-to, pinning my hand behind my back. With his other hand, he grasped my second wrist. My chest heaved with impotent anger and fear, and the room fairly spun with the intensity of my feelings. And before I knew what was happening, his mouth met mine.

I wanted to protest. I wanted to push him away.

I wanted to be stronger than I was.

But I was not. As he kissed me, I moaned. My wrists pinned helplessly behind my back, overcome by the sheer size of the man compared to my tiny frame, I felt consumed by him. His mouth was warm and sensual, surprisingly soft, and in sharp contrast to the whiskers that pricked my lips. I felt the flicker of his tongue in my mouth, and my chest constricted, as he kept his hands firmly on mine. He kissed me until my knees weakened. I'd never been kissed like this before.

I heard the distant chirping of the birds, and further in the distance, the bang of an axe on a log. Someone was chopping wood, and a hawk cried overhead, but it all murmured in the background as my only focus was Samuel's mouth on mine. Arousal flamed in me, licks of fire between my legs and low in my belly, as my body yearned to be touched by him.

I'd been sold into marriage by my father to a man who beat me on our wedding night and took what he wanted. I'd never been touched by a lover before. I longed for Samuel's touch. I wanted more, as I felt deep within me that somehow his touch would cleanse me. I wanted his hands on my breasts. I wanted him to strip me. I wanted his strong, powerful hands over my bare skin, ravishing me as I relinquished myself to him so that my body no longer remembered the savage assault I'd experienced, but instead the claiming of a real man, a lover.

I knew my thoughts were wanton. I well knew that such desires for an unwed woman were considered sinful. Other than the Stanleys, 'polite society' had spurned me when I'd been wed to a man who drank and beat me, so I'd long since discarded any care for societal expectations and morals.

As his mouth pulled away from me, I looked at him in astonishment. I had no words.

His eyes smiled at me. "I have means to quiet that razor-sharp tongue of yours, little Ruth."

"You're a brute," I whispered helplessly.

He released my hands and stepped back, one corner of his mouth turning up. "Honey, if you think that was brutal, we could have a talk or two to show you otherwise."

And in that moment, somehow it all struck me as funny. My flaring temper, over—what? His 'way' of quieting my mouth. His declaration that I needed a spanking but he'd stay his hand, and the way he implied he could do more than kiss me to keep me in line. Amusement bubbled up inside me that I couldn't contain. I put a hand to my mouth and laughed. His eyes widened. The laughter burst out of me and I snorted out loud. He looked astonished, even as his eyes darkened. I found it hilarious.

"You'd quiet my mouth with a kiss?" I asked, in between gasps of breath. "You were mad enough to swallow a horned toad backwards!"

His mouth dropped open.

"Oh, I'm simply shaking with fright!" I guffawed, not sure where I was going with this, but certain that if my punishment for provocation had been a kiss like that, I needed to provoke him again.

"Woman," he warned, but I would not be quieted.

"And I'd like to see you try to spank me, Samuel Stanley! I'll tell your ma on you!"

His eyes were dark now. "She'd clap my back and congratulate me," he growled.

This had me howling with laughter.

I didn't know such a large man could move so quickly. He had me cornered, then up and over his shoulder in seconds, marching me out of Hannah's bedroom and into the main room of the cabin. I protested, of course, but it was no use and I knew it. He walked with decided steps to my room and tossed me down on the bed.

I shrieked with laughter. "Oh, you look like a bear that's just emerged from his winter cave, with those eyes of yours," I taunted. I placed the back of my hand to my forehead and pretended to be faint. "What's a girl to do?"

"Stop your yappin'!"

I needed him to kiss me, or spank me, I just needed him to *touch* me, and I needed him to touch me *now*.

"Yap yap *yap*!" I prattled on. He growled, bending down toward me again, lowering his mouth close to my ear as he grasped my bottom with one hand and squeezed. It was a shocking gesture, scandalous for an unmarried couple.

"Naughty little Ruth needs to be put in her place."

He kissed me again, and this time, his hands roved my body. I moaned into his mouth, my hands on his chest, my palms flat against his shirt. I could feel the hardened muscles

15

beneath, and I shifted with arousal.

He wrenched his mouth off mine, but only to growl one more warning. "Are you gonna behave yourself now, or not?"

"Nooooo," I moaned, as I did not want this to stop. I began unfastening the buttons on his shirt. He removed it as the last button came undone. I stared for a moment at his muscled chest, honed by years of hard labor. As I roamed my hands across the sprinkling of hair and lower still to the taut muscles, I could see the evidence of his arousal tented in his trousers. I felt suddenly overcome with tears.

He wanted me.

Until then, I'd never been desired like *this*, in a way that made me feel attractive and beautiful. With my husband, I was merely a vessel for him to use to satisfy his base desires. But for Samuel, it was different. He hungered for me even his firmest touches were gentle. Right then, I'd have allowed him to have his way with me. I'd have refused him nothing.

"You beautiful, reckless, naughty little girl," he whispered in my ear.

"I'm not a girl," I replied in protest.

"When you're with me you are."

My lady parts tingled as one large hand wrapped around my waist and pulled me closer to him. His mouth on mine again, we kissed as his hand kneaded my breast, one firm thumb encircling my nipples straight through the fabric.

I knew I should have protested. I should have insisted he court me, or sent him on his way. But I did not care that we were not married. Samuel made me feel wanted for the first time in my life, and I yearned for more.

I was pinned beneath him now as he kissed me, bracing himself over me with one hand so he wouldn't smother me, while the other was hiking up my skirts. My thighs clenched together in anticipation as I felt the warmth of his hand on my stocking. Blast the layers of clothing I was wearing! He smoothed a hand over my drawers. My hips bucked. The intensity of my arousal had me near tears.

"Please," I begged, conscious of the desperation in my voice.

"Sit up," he ordered. "Undress yourself."

Hastily I obeyed, until I was wearing nothing but a thin chemise and drawers.

"Ah, so you *will* obey," he said. "Seems I may have found the key."

I moaned in reply as he laid me back down, lowering himself over me again, his lips insistent and probing. He kissed me as he pulled my drawers down, dipping a finger between my legs to my most sensitive parts. My breath caught in my throat as he stroked me. The feeling was exquisite.

"Spread your legs, honey," he whispered. I obeyed, while he stroked me, his other arm holding me close to him while we kissed. Two fingers plunged into my core. I gasped from the sheer pleasure before he went back, stroking me. I was going to lose control, with Samuel holding me tightly next to him. In minutes, the release coursed through me, waves of ecstasy meeting in a delicious crescendo as he stroked and pumped my sex. He kissed me slowly, softly, holding me until the delicious spasms passed.

"You feelin' better?" he whispered.

"Yes," I replied with a sigh. "You?"

He chuckled. "No, but that'll be for another day. Today was about puttin' you in your place."

I pursed my lips. "Is that so?"

"It is. You'll question me now, woman?" he said with a raised brow.

I smiled. "No, sir," I said, as meekly as a lamb.

"Sir, is it?" he said. "I'm not sure you've called me that before."

"No, sir," I said, closing my eyes as he lowered himself onto the bed next to me.

He chuckled. "Now are you gonna be a good girl, get yourself dressed, and come bake me one of your cakes, or am I gonna have to toss you over my shoulder and carry you on over?"

"You and your taunts," I muttered. "Toss you over your shoulder! Spank your naughty little bottom!"

He tilted a head to me. Though his eyes twinkled, his voice was stern. "Oh, honey, those weren't threats. Now get yourself dressed and let's go before I prove that to you."

Not in the mood to test him, subdued after he'd brought me to ecstasy, I obeyed.

CHAPTER TWO: TOSSED INTO A LOFT

I dressed, while Samuel righted himself and went out to the barn to do some of my morning chores. I left the birds with water and some grubs, and fixed my hair. I looked a right mess after he'd laid me down in bed. My cheeks flamed with embarrassment as I remembered lying in bed next to him. And it wasn't just because of his intimate touch. No, it was deeper than that. I had been a docile lamb afterwards.

Yes, sir.

I closed my eyes, pursing my lips as I splashed cold water on my face and tidied up. I'd been beaten by my husband and mistreated by my father, but I'd never willingly submitted to any man. I sure wasn't going to start now. I was a woman in my own right, and I'd stay that way.

Samuel came in a few minutes later, tapping off his boots and shaking off his hat, hanging it up on a peg. "You ready to go?" he asked.

"In a minute," I said. "I have a few things to tend to. Why don't you go on up ahead and I'll meet you in a little while?"

He frowned. "You think I'm leaving you to travel alone when I'm right here, and can go with you? Nonsense, woman. Do what you need to, then we'll go." He turned his back to me, pulled a chair out, and sat down. Well, then.

I didn't need to worry about cooking, since I'd be with Ma for most of the day, but I did need to set my sourdough bread to fermenting. I affixed my apron and busied myself flitting around the kitchen, turning out my flour and deftly preparing the dough.

"That's astoundin'," Samuel murmured. I paused, flour straight up to my elbows, and looked at him.

"What is?"

"The way you just—" His hands flipped around and twisted. "And then you just—" He pretended to pat the dough. I smiled.

"You never seen a woman prepare dough before?" I asked, incredulous. He was around enough women in the Stanley line to know that this was routine. I was puzzled. But he was staring at my hands now. He sat with his legs spread apart, hands folded lightly in his lap. His voice was low and husky when he spoke.

"Not with pretty little hands like that, I haven't."

My lady parts well remembered where his hands had been. I squirmed.

"Land's sake," I whispered. "Samuel, you've one mind!"

He chuckled low. "Ain't that the truth."

"And blast if I can't keep my head on straight around you acting like that," I muttered.

He grinned. "Well, now. I'll keep that in mind. Maybe I can keep little Ruth behavin' herself for another minute or two."

I flicked flour from my fingers at him, which merely elicited a low, manly chuckle I felt down to my bones. Oh, this wouldn't do at all.

"Behave *yourself*," I hissed, momentarily forgetting what to do with the dough next. Another chuckle.

"Or what?" he teased, drawing his arms up and crossing them over his broad chest as he sat up. "You'll raise your little voice to me?" He was taunting me now, lips pursed and eyes twinkling.

I glared at him and lifted my chin. "Behave, or I won't let you kiss me again."

He grinned, but his voice was low as he leaned forward, speaking in a measured tone. "I'd like to see you try to stop me."

I gave the bread dough a sound slap that reverberated around the cabin. He shook his head, rising to his feet, as I finished up my preparations and wiped my hands on my apron.

"Come now, woman," he said. He took my hand, and I felt my heart flutter in my chest. I loved the feeling of his hand in mine. But as we walked together toward his home, I wondered. What had changed between the two of us? Where did we go from here?

• • • • • • •

I spent the morning doing chores with Ma. My honey cake looked simply decadent sitting atop her glass plate, drizzled with warm, golden goodness. Buckets full of honey stood ready to take back to my own home, and Pearl and Geraldine came to fetch some, too. The honey tree had been a veritable goldmine.

Arriving before Geraldine, Pearl gave me a big hug around the neck and a peck on my cheek. "Oh, it's good to see you," she said, her blue eyes shining at me. She was a pretty thing, taller and fuller than I was, her dark, unruly hair tucked into a thick bun with wisps of curls framing her face. She had a fetching smattering of freckles around her nose, and her eyes were shining. Pearl was expecting a baby in the summer, and her face was fuller and rounder, simply glowing. I placed a hand on her swollen belly and smiled at her.

"How's young little Aaron?" I asked her. She smiled. We had already decided that Pearl was having a baby boy, and that if she ended up with a girl, it was only because Aaron had changed his mind. He was the bossy sort, so I liked to tease her that the baby would be a little Aaron.

"Not Aaron," Pearl said with a roll of her eyes. We had this conversation at least several times a week. "Behave yourself, Ruth. His name is *Patrick*."

"If you say so," I said. "Seems fitting that he'd be named after a man that drove the snakes from Ireland."

Ma chuckled behind me. She knew I'd devoured every one of the books that were her husband's, tucked away on the little shelf by the fire, and regularly clucked her tongue at me when I would pull out an odd fact or anecdote. Sweet as she was, Ma had no use for fables and stories. She'd been raised by strict Methodist parents, and now only allowed fiction in her home out of respect for her late husband. I'd been told he not only allowed novels to be read, but would read aloud to his whole family by the fire.

Geraldine snorted in the background. "Those stories are for heathens, Ruth. You ought to keep your head away from them and focus on real life instead."

Ma's lips pursed as she swept the floor. "My husband didn't abide heathen tales, Geraldine. Now you hold your tongue." We all knew how Ma felt about the novels herself, but it was an insult to her late husband's wishes to criticize, and we all knew it. I merely buttoned my lip and continued stewing the chicken in the pot on the stove. I watched Pearl. Pearl looked intently at Geraldine before she turned away. I knew she wasn't allowed to engage in arguments, though she could have a sharp tongue herself, and had no qualms about standing up to Geraldine. I could tell she was trying to decide if it was worth contradicting Geraldine. Apparently, she'd decided not to.

Pearl's marriage to Aaron only the year before had surprised the Stanley family. Samuel told me the story of how the brothers had joined a band of travelers heading west. They'd rescued Pearl from the home she'd been staying in as a servant, as she was the lone survivor in a late-night raid. I loved Pearl's story of rescue, and I loved watching her with her husband. I'd not known many married couples, and none who were as affectionate as Aaron and Pearl.

I liked Pearl. Like me, she'd known a troubled childhood. Details would surface when we worked side by side. We'd picked beans together one day, and she told me how she'd been raised by a couple that had taken her in and treated her like a slave.

"Before I met Aaron, I never knew what it was like to be happy," she said.

I hadn't responded at the time, because I still wondered what that would be like. I'd never known either.

Pearl knew what it was like to be unwanted and unloved. She was every bit an adopted member of the Stanley family as I was, only she was actually a member. I was not.

Geraldine was another story.

She was shorter and smaller than Pearl but taller than I was. That didn't really account for much, though, because everyone was taller than I was, even Samuel's brother Matthew. Geraldine was neat as a pin and lovely, her gleaming chestnut hair always immaculate, her skin smooth as silk. I envied her hair when I was tucking away my own dark tresses in a bun. She was a bit plumper now than when I first met her, and carried her wee one on her arm. Her eyes were shrewd and distant, and though Pearl said Geraldine was much kinder now than when she'd first met her, I found it hard to believe. We did not much care for one another and kept a respectful distance. If I hadn't had so much respect for Ma, on more than one occasion, I'd have let Geraldine have a piece of my mind.

As I stewed the chicken, I mulled over how I'd been bested by Samuel. I felt irritable and cross, in no mood to deal with Geraldine's haughty ways.

By noon, Ma and I were busily finishing up our preparations. Geraldine and Pearl were to the side, by the fire, Pearl knitting a pair of booties for Geraldine's little Mary Jane. Geraldine sat with her baby, and I almost, for a brief minute, softened to the woman. I'd heard whispered stories about her having lost several babies before she'd given birth, and at least one—maybe more—she'd delivered and lost. I knew she had a handful of tiny, shallow graves she visited. It was the harsh reality we accepted, though I'd never lost a baby.

But at the moment, as I looked to Geraldine, with her perfectly smooth hair and immaculate complexion, her straight-as-an-arrow spine and haughty air, I was not feeling any sympathy. I was still fuming about her dismissal of the books I liked to read. I longed to see her firmly put in her place.

"How's the chicken coming along, child?" Ma murmured next to me.

"Quite nicely," I said. Ma had beans and cornbread ready for the men when they came for dinner, but the chicken and biscuits would serve us all that evening. I looked forward eagerly to the meal, and not just because I enjoyed chicken and craved the taste of meat again. I loved being surrounded by the whole extended Stanley family. Geraldine typically behaved herself better when Phillip was around.

"Be sure there are no bones, Ruth," Geraldine said from the fire. Ma pursed her lips, but it was Pearl who spoke. Her eyes never left her hands, her knitting sitting atop her ample belly.

"No one cooks a finer chicken than Ruth, Geraldine," she said. "If you got a bone, it was likely a message to you from above."

Ma's eyes twinkled but she kept her own counsel. I, on the other hand, could not keep my temper at bay any longer.

"If you don't like how I cook, you can cook your own damn food. No one's forcing you to eat what I make." I heard Ma gasp beside me and Pearl's eyes lifted from her knitting, widening. Geraldine scowled. She sat with her baby over her shoulder, patting her back as she dozed.

"No need for you to get your petticoats in a bunch," Geraldine snapped.

"Girls," Ma chided, as she made her way to the door.

"You behave yourselves. I'm going to pick some daisies for our dinner table." She loved flowers, and was always adorning the inside of her home with the wild violets, daisies, and even dandelions that scattered like pebbles by the lake across our wide, open prairie. I waited until she stepped out before I spoke.

"I'm behaving myself just fine," I said, stirring the chicken so hard it splattered over the edge of the pot and hissed on the hot stove. "It's this one over here with a mouth the size of a full moon that won't stop."

Geraldine stood. Handing her baby to Pearl, she marched over to me with her hands on her hips and her eyes flashing.

"How *dare* you call me names?" she hissed. Her eyes were bright and angry, her cheeks pink. She waved a finger in front of me as I turned and faced her. Granted, I had to look up to her, given that I was that much shorter, but what I lacked in stature I made up for in vim and vigor.

"How dare *you* criticize my cooking and tell me what to do?" I replied, my voice rising.

"Please!" Pearl begged from where she sat with the baby. Geraldine took her hands off her hips and stepped closer to me. Without thinking, I grabbed the cup of water I had next to the pot of chicken, as I'd splash a bit in if necessary, and tossed the whole cup right into her furious face.

She screamed. I felt a thrill of victory run through me. Pearl gasped. Geraldine's hair was dripping wet, and she looked fit to be tied. Would she hurt me? I was ready. But we never did know, for it was at that moment the men came in from the fields.

I heard Phillip first. "Whoa! What's goin' on in here?" he asked, as he rushed to Geraldine, pulling her away from me and closer to where the table was.

"She threw a glass of water in my face!" Geraldine shrieked, a shaky finger waving at me.

"She deserved it!" I said angrily, turning, unrepentant, back to the stove. "Making fun of me. Started out calling me

25

names and saying I was a heathen for reading books that were your *father's*, which personally I think is a crying shame. Second, telling me I don't know how to cook. She wouldn't close her mouth, so I closed it—"

"Ruth."

One word. Deep, laced with disapproval, I knew it well. I turned. Samuel stood in the doorway, and Aaron, the eldest of the Stanley brothers who looked remarkably like Samuel, not far behind him. I sighed. My conscience began to prick me. Ma wanted me to keep the peace, and I wasn't welcome to cause discord. I didn't want to. I loved this family.

Still, I was not obedient to Samuel and he wasn't going to make me obey.

I quietly stirred the chicken. But he was not done.

"You put that spoon down. Pearl? Hand the baby to Geraldine, please, and you continue with the dinner. Ruth and I need to step outside for a few minutes."

"I'm almost done," I said. I didn't like the idea of being corrected in front of a room full of people, and I wasn't exactly sure what he would do with me when we were alone. But when the man put his mind to something, he would not be dissuaded.

"*Now.*"

I did not want to obey, but I also didn't want to cause another scene. With a sigh, I handed the spoon to Pearl. She gave me a sympathetic look and a peck on the cheek, leaning in and whispering to me, "She had that coming. He's a gentle sort, Ruth. You know that. Just take a breath of fresh air outside."

I was trying to find a way to exit gracefully, but he had me by the elbow, marching in firm strides to the doorway. It angered me. I pulled my elbow out of his grasp and spun away. He was fast; one hand wrapped around my waist before I could get two steps away, his mouth by my ear. "You walk with me now, or I'll carry you out. Your choice."

I swallowed, facing him angrily. I pulled away and

marched to the door. Now I wanted to get away from *all* of them. Aaron stepped aside so I could storm past him. I could see Ma approaching us now. Guilt pricked my conscience.

She didn't like when I lost my temper. I was in her home. I'd been wrong.

Samuel stood by my side, still holding my elbow. As Ma approached us, she glanced at his hand on me.

"Don't wait dinner for us, please," Samuel said. Ma's eyes grew concerned.

"Everything all right?" she asked.

"It will be."

Her eyes went from his to mine before she nodded. "Right, then. See you soon."

I was grateful that she kept her own counsel. After she left, Samuel walked with firm, deliberate steps to the barn. Now that we were alone, my mind teemed with questions. Why there? What would he do? My heart began to stutter in my chest, and I began to tremble. There was no escaping. I had misbehaved, and he was not going to tolerate it. But what would that entail? The memory of his stating I needed a spanking echoed in my mind.

When we got to the barn, he took me to a large, private area and released my elbow. I stepped away from him and glared. I didn't like being hauled to the barn like a naughty child.

Samuel crossed his arms on his chest, his eyes stern and inflexible. His lips thinned, and his voice was curt. "Tell me what happened. If you run, I'll catch you and you'll wish I hadn't."

Continuing to glare silently, I crossed my arms and stared at him.

His voice softened a bit. "Ruth, I want to hear your side of the story."

He was not judging. He was not criticizing. He'd given me space to talk, and wanted to understand what was going on.

I took a deep breath and tried. "Well, that good for nothing—"

"No. Tell me what *you* did and why."

Though I knew my actions were childish, and I disliked having caused dissension, I was unrepentant. I *would* tell the story my way.

"Geraldine poked fun at me. She does it all the time, to both me and Pearl. Thinks she is better than us, and that she has the right to demean us. And I'll not put up with it, Samuel. I *won't!*"

A muscle twitched in his jaw. He was still wearing his wide-brimmed hat, which caused a slight shadow to darken his eyes. "Did I ask you what she did, little Ruth? Or did I ask you to tell me what *you* did?"

"It's the same!" I said, throwing my hands up in anger.

He sighed. "All right, then. What happened *today*, young lady?"

There it was again: young lady. Only for some reason, this time it made me feel a twinge of guilt. "I... she said I read heathen books. I referenced Saint Patrick making the snakes leave Ireland. It was in your *father's* book I read, and she has no right—"

"Ruth."

I sighed. "And then she had the nerve to tell me to be sure there were no chicken bones in our supper."

He nodded. "Go on."

I suddenly felt very small. "I... well. That was it."

His brows shot up in surprise. "She said you read a heathen book, and asked you to be sure there were no bones in the chicken? And you thought that reason to toss water in her face? To provoke my brother's wife?"

His tone of voice stoked my barely tempered fire and I stepped toward him, my chest heaving with anger. "Don't you *dare* take her side!" I hissed.

Though he moved quickly, it seemed later that it was all in slow motion. The way his arms uncrossed and his large hand came to my jaw, grasping me firmly, tilting my face up to his. The way his eyes narrowed and heated. Grasping me gently but firmly, he made me look into his eyes.

"Woman, hold your tongue," he whispered. I yanked my face away from him and shoved him back. In seconds, strong arms wrapped around my torso, and though I fought with all my strength, he was so much stronger than I, he could've bested me with one arm tied behind his back. He lifted me clear off the ground, and to my shock, fairly tossed me over his head, where I landed on a bed of soft hay. He'd put me straight into the loft.

It was a low-hanging loft, much lower than the typical ones in barns in our little town, and it served as a sort of storage place for Ma. She was small, like me, and could easily reach atop it without having to climb the taller ladder on the other side of the barn. So there I sat, tumbled in the hay, Samuel just below. His hands grasped the edge.

"Little Ruth, I've already explained that if your past was different, I'd have taken you across my knee long ago. But woman, does my palm ever itch to tan your backside."

I scrambled to the edge of the loft, but his voice made me freeze. "You've been warned, young lady. You get down from that loft before I give you leave, and past be damned, I'll toss you over my lap, lift your skirts, and spank you until you beg me for mercy. Understand?"

I paused. I was angry at my inability to control the situation, yet still attracted to his strength. Not knowing what else to do, I crossed my arms angrily. I wanted to fight him. I wanted to push him. I didn't like the torrent of emotions within me. My skin felt like it was on fire, prickles of nerves making me feel near desperate. And as I sat in the loft, feeling sorry for myself and ashamed of my behavior, I realized something else.

I wanted him to spank me.

I wanted to feel helpless. I wanted *him* to take control. I needed to know he cared enough about me that he wouldn't allow me to act like a child. I yearned for his touch on my naked skin.

But wild horses wouldn't drag the truth from me.

I was furious with my choices. Cow to his demands and stay put in the loft, or go down and get a spanking. Though part of me wanted the spanking, I felt getting down from the loft would give him the upper hand; if not when I got first down, for certain when I was sprawled over his lap. I didn't want to submit.

So I sat down on the hay. He pulled a stout milking stool from another stall, plunked it in front of the wall, and sat down across from me. His eyes never left mine. I heaved with fury, but refused to get down, which made me even angrier because he was winning the battle of wills.

"It's not fair," I spat out, my voice high and tight with anger.

His voice was even and low when he spoke. "What's not fair?"

"You all let her get away with being a mean, spiteful witch." I felt tears prick the back of my eyes and my throat felt tight. I hated when people were mean.

"Not sure what you mean by 'get away with it,'" he said. "I don't allow her to backtalk to me, and Aaron stands up to her if she's rude to Pearl. But there ain't much more in our control. If she were mine, it'd be a different story, but I'll not tell my brother how to run his household."

I flopped belly down on the hay and placed my chin in my hands. He had a point. But what he said saddened me, and I wasn't sure why. I thought over what he'd said for a minute.

Samuel didn't allow her to be rude to him.

Aaron defended Pearl.

Who would defend *me*? It wasn't fair. The hurt I felt deflated my anger, and I no longer wished to speak of it. I sighed and put my head on my arms, closing my eyes. I didn't want him to see me cry. After a few moments, Samuel spoke, and his voice had softened.

"Ruth?"

I opened my eyes. "Yes?" I asked.

"What's on your mind?"

I decided there was no harm in telling him the truth. "You said Aaron defends Pearl. Well, that's wonderful, *if you're Pearl*. But if you're me? With no one to defend you? And you defend *yourself*? You get tossed into a loft and threatened with spanking." My voice caught. I would not let him see me cry. I would *not*!

I turned from him, then, and faced the other end of the loft. I suddenly felt very, very tired. I placed my head on my arms and closed my eyes. I felt the heaviness begin to settle on my chest, the weight I felt most days, squeezing my heart and making my head feel stuffy. I rarely cried. I simply carried on, doing what I had to do, bearing my yoke without complaint. My burden was heavy. And if no one would help me lift it, I would carry it myself.

I heard his steady breathing, and the comforting sounds of the animals in the barn, the shifting hooves of the horses, and the soft nuzzles and chewing sounds on the other side of the wall. The hay smelled sweet and the barn was warm. My eyes as heavy as the rest of me, I fell asleep.

• • • • • • •

When I woke, the barn had darkened a bit. I wondered how long I'd been asleep, and I sat up with a start, momentarily forgetting where I was, and why. I looked over to where Samuel had been sitting. He was still there, his saddle upon his knee. He had a small tin of oil and a rag, and was cleaning it thoroughly. Next to him sat his rifle and stout riding quirt. He'd kept himself busy while I slept, tending to his tools.

"Feelin' better, little Ruth?" he asked. I felt shy watching him as he sat atop the stool, his large legs spread apart and the leather saddle straddling one knee, his hat still atop his head and shadowing his stubbled jaw.

"I think so," I said quietly. "Samuel?" I sat up and rubbed a hand across my eyes, my fingers nimbly fixing my hair.

He stilled, his blue eyes coming to mine, placid and tender. "Yes, honey?"

I loved when he called me honey. I swallowed. "Have you been sitting here the whole time?" I asked.

He smiled gently. "About when I figured out you weren't comin' down and I wouldn't have to snatch you up and warm your bottom, I got my tools, came back here, and have been workin' ever since. You feelin' less ornery?"

"I am," I said, though the sorrow from earlier still lingered. "Now will you let me down?"

He placed his saddle down and rose, unfolding his large frame, every inch of him raw, bridled strength. He crossed the distance between us in two long strides, and I felt the energy between us crackle as he got closer, my need to have him touch me intensifying.

He reached his hands out to me. "Come, now, little Ruth," he said. I could've simply slid off the edge, but he was having none of it. He reached one hand under my arms and the other under my legs, swung me up and over the edge, but he didn't release me right away.

"You've got a pattern of straw on your cheek," he said with a chuckle. Up close to his chest like this, I felt his deep voice down to my toes. I remembered the feel of his hands on my intimate parts, roaming my body, and my mouth grew dry. My latent desire renewed. To my immense pleasure he bent down and kissed my cheek. His warm mouth on my skin was welcome, his whiskers prickled, and I wished it was my mouth, not my cheek, that he kissed.

At the doorway to the barn, he let me down. I knew he had to, though I wanted to be held longer. I felt warmth in my cheeks and in my chest, arousal pulsing low between my legs. After years of neglecting my womanly needs, the attraction to Samuel was almost disconcerting. I had been so removed from my attraction to men that it felt new, more powerful, and a bit unwelcome. I wasn't quite sure how to handle it.

"Matthew and Hannah are due from school soon, and Aaron's gone to fetch them. You go on in the cabin with Ma, and see to helping her." He reached for my hand and squeezed it. "And Ruth?"

I nodded, feeling meeker than I had in a good long while.

His eyes darkened and his lips thinned. "If Geraldine is ornery, you fetch me. I'll not be far today. You stay out of her way as much as you can, but if she lights into you, you let me handle her. Will you do that?"

In the past, even a week or so ago, I'd have refused his offer. I'd have insisted I could fend for myself. I felt just a bit of the heaviness about me lift, just a little, as I nodded my consent.

"Good girl," he said, granting me one of his rare grins. He took my hand to his lips and kissed my fingers. I watched him go, and I missed him already.

When I returned to the cabin, there was no need to worry about Geraldine. She was calm and placid. Pearl lifted curious eyes to me, as if to make sure I was unharmed, then she returned to her work. Ma welcomed me back as if I hadn't been taken to the barn and then gone for hours. I wondered what they suspected. Did they wonder if he'd punished me? Though Samuel was the gentlest of the Stanley brothers, he came from a line of stern, rugged men who were decidedly in charge, and unapologetic in their expectation of obedience. I'd heard a few stories about Aaron and Pearl, and I also knew that Ma frequently said that her own boys had inherited the same traits from their pa. But everyone kept their own counsel.

Ma had a pile of wild mustard and dandelion greens we'd boil as our first spring vegetable dish. They needed to be sorted, picked through, and cleaned. Geraldine was busy once again rocking her baby and trying to get her to sleep, Pearl was knitting placidly, and I was sitting by the table, when the door flung open. Samuel stood in the doorway, his eyes serious, and I started at the sudden appearance.

"Ruth, come with me," he said. I got to my feet, feeling

the dread pool in my stomach. Something was horribly wrong.

"What is it?" I whispered.

"Hannah's had a fall," he said. "Aaron sent word with Matthew for me to fetch you, and Phillip's gone for the doctor. Come now, woman."

I fled the cabin, instinctively reaching for his hand, nearly running to keep up with his long strides. When we reached his horse, he put his hands on my waist and lifted me. I sat side-saddle while he heaved himself up. Wrapping my arms around his back, I held on tightly as he galloped toward home.

CHAPTER THREE: TEMPER BREWING

We rode in silence, the only sound the thundering of Trigger's hooves on the hard prairie grass, and my heartbeat hammering against Samuel's back. What had happened? I had seen my little girl hurt, and I could hardly bear it. I'd have gladly offered myself in place of her, and had, many times. She'd experienced too much in her tender years, and she needed no more harm to come to her. As we rode across the prairie, my heart squeezed in my chest, and I felt it difficult to breathe. I concentrated on feeling the roughness of Samuel's shirt beneath my fingers, his hardened muscles beneath the fabric, and watching his strong, capable hands holding the reins. He was an accomplished rider, and he led Trigger with ease over the bumpy terrain. In no time at all, we arrived at my home.

Samuel slung himself down from his horse and I tried to shimmy myself down, so eager was I to get to Hannah, but Samuel's growl stopped me. I frowned at him, but allowed him to help me down, his hands around my waist, but when my feet hit the ground, I was already running. I yanked the door to our cabin, rushing inside. Aaron stood in the main area of the cabin, leaning against the table with his arms crossed, and Matthew was pacing in front of the fireplace.

"What happened?" I asked. "Where's Hannah?"

Matthew looked down sheepishly. "She's in her room," he said, jerking a finger behind him. I wondered if it was a foolhardy scheme of his that got Hannah hurt, but I didn't pause for an explanation; instead, rushing into Hannah's room, with Samuel right behind me and Aaron following. Matthew hung by the door.

"Ma!" Hannah said weakly as I rushed to her side. The doctor was holding her left arm and examining her carefully. I took Hannah's uninjured hand.

Dr. Gentry was an older man, with white hair and a white mustache, his golden spectacles perched atop his nose. His typically jovial face looked grim as he examined Hannah.

"Seems these two young 'uns were having a tree-climbin' contest," he said, his voice heavy with rebuke. "Fortunately, it looks as if there's no breakage, but a serious sprain. She'll have no use of the arm for a few weeks, and we'll keep it tied up in a sling. She's fortunate that she didn't do more damage. Falls like hers often result in far worse injuries, even a broken neck." I inhaled sharply. My girl!

Matthew shifted in the doorway. He looked down at the floor. "It was my idea and it was stupid," he muttered. Aaron and Samuel looked over at him.

I turned back to Hannah and raised my brows. She nodded sheepishly.

"I didn't want to be bested by him," she said. "He told me girls can't climb as high in a dress, and I wanted to show him he was wrong." Her eyes flashed. I sighed. My girl was a spitfire.

"Well, Matthew isn't the one lying here in bed," I chided. "Seems he *did* best you, then." I knew the knowledge that he'd won the contest would be punishing enough for her, and she'd remember the loss every time she went to use her arm over the next few weeks. Hannah frowned.

Aaron walked to the door. "Seems you all have this situation under control. I need to get back to Pearl. It's suppertime, and she's often tired in the evenin'.'" He tipped his hat to me.

"Thank you, Aaron," I said. "You were the one who helped her get back here?" I smiled my thanks.

He nodded. "Matthew was doing his best on his own, but I had my horse. We got her back here, then Matthew was the one to fetch the doctor."

"Thank you, Matthew," I said.

Samuel, however, was frowning.

Aaron turned to Samuel and Matthew. "You'll see to Matthew getting home, then?" he asked.

"I will," Samuel said shortly. Aaron tipped his hat again and left.

As Dr. Gentry tied a sling around Hannah's arm, Samuel spoke to Matthew. "You see that girl laid up in pain because of your foolhardy behavior?" he asked sharply.

Matthew shifted. "Yes, sir."

Samuel's eyes smoldered. "You're older than she is, bigger, and stronger. And you're a man. Men are supposed to protect and care for women, not lead them into danger."

"Yes, sir. I know'd it," Matthew said, kicking a toe of his shoe into the floorboard.

Samuel gave him a long, hard look, his hands placed firmly on his hips. "How do you think you'll make amends for what happened today?"

Matthew looked embarrassed, but to his credit, looked at his brother steadily. "You're askin' *me*?"

Samuel nodded. "I am."

I felt sorry for Matthew, and didn't want to see him in too much trouble, especially when he already felt so bad. "Samuel, seeing as Hannah's injuries will prevent her from doing her chores properly around here, wouldn't it be more fitting for him to help her out?"

Matthew frowned. "I'd rather take a whuppin'," he muttered, kicking at the floor again. Samuel's eyes met mine across the room and smiled at me.

"Seems doing her chores while she's laid up would be

proper, then," Samuel said. "What are Hannah's evening chores?"

After I'd detailed her responsibilities, Samuel took Matthew out to the barn to do Hannah's chores while Dr. Gentry faced me. "She'll be fine in a few weeks, if she rests properly," he explained, but his eyes went back to Hannah's. "No heavy lifting, or tree climbing, or anything of the sort. You hear me, Hannah?"

Hannah nodded soberly. I thanked the doctor as we walked to the door.

"Well, now, it's my pleasure, Ruth," he said calmly. There had been more than one occasion when Dr. Gentry had tended to me and Hannah after we'd been hurt by my late husband. I knew him to be fair and gentle, but to respect our privacy as well.

"Dr. Gentry, I have no way to pay you," I said. Dr. Gentry was a widower with no children, and lived alone in town. Being the town doctor to a crowd of hard-working, but rather poor farmers, made his job less than profitable.

He waved a hand. "Now, Ruth, I'd not be taking money from you for such a small injury. I merely tied a sling and examined her."

"Some of my berry preserves, then?" I asked, going to our pantry and extracting a vibrant red jar of raspberry jam, my favorite. I did make delicious jam.

"That'd be more than enough," he said, taking the proffered payment with a smile. As he left, I looked out to the barn, where Samuel and Matthew were. Matthew came to the doorway, and Dr. Gentry spoke with Samuel for a moment. There were nods and waves, and to my surprise, I saw Matthew get atop Dr. Gentry's horse, and the two of them rode away together. My heart thumped. I wondered if that meant Samuel was staying longer.

My heart beat steadily in my chest as I saw Samuel tip his hat to Matthew and Dr. Gentry, before heading to me with long, purposeful strides.

I turned tail and scurried back to Hannah, who was

trying to get up out of bed.

"Oh, no, you don't," I said firmly. "You scoot yourself back in bed."

"But Ma! I'm fine," Hannah protested. "It's just my arm, and the rest of me is just the same as usual. I can still get up and walk about. And when did you bring those birds in?"

"As for the little birds, I brought them in this morning. Their mama... well, the birds need us to provide for them. As for you, I'll have you stay in bed tonight."

"I promise I'm fine," she protested, but I heard Samuel come in behind me.

"You mind your ma," he said, with quiet rebuke, as he walked over to Hannah's side.

Hannah's eyes widened, but she merely nodded up at him.

He continued. "After a good night's sleep, we'll see how you're doin' tomorrow." He gently stroked the hair back from her forehead, and I warmed at that. "You best get yourself better now, darlin', if you want to go fishin' with me and Matthew like we talked about. If you're better tomorrow, we'll decide if we'll let you up out of bed."

We.

The way he joined me in a decision having to do with my daughter's well-being touched me. I closed my eyes momentarily, overcome with the emotion of the day. It had been such a very, very long day.

As Hannah's head rested back on her pillow, I saw how weary she was, too. She nodded to Samuel. "Yes, sir."

"I'll fetch you some supper, sweetheart," I murmured, tucking a stray lock of hair behind her ear. She nodded, and her eyes closed.

"Yes, ma'am."

Samuel joined me in the main area of the cabin. "Where'd Matthew go?" I asked as I scurried around, frying up eggs and slicing bread.

"Dr. Gentry had to see Ma and return some of her empty jars," he explained. "So he said he'd take Matthew home."

I nodded, pushing a plate of food in front of Samuel, and a second plate next to his. I went to Hannah's room with food and a cool tin cup of milk, but when I got there, I heard her light snores and heavy breathing. I stood by her bed, watching her sleep for a moment, smoothing her hair back off her forehead and tucking her blanket a bit tighter around her. She'd have to remove her dress and prepare to sleep, but I didn't want to wake her yet. I would let her rest.

I wanted to put my arms around her and draw her to me, hold her tight, and not let anyone or anything ever hurt her again. I looked over at the nest still on the little table by her window, and the softly sleeping forms of the tiny little birds. I knew that one day, the day when those little birds would grow old enough to fly on their own, they would have to be set free. I looked at my little Hannah. Letting her fly alone meant she risked being hurt. I couldn't bear to think about it. I needed her by my side, where I could watch and protect her.

After smoothing the blanket over her one last time, I went back to Samuel. He was still sitting in front of his untouched food.

"Land's sake, Samuel, what are you waiting for? Tuck in," I said.

He lifted his brows to me. "Bossin' me around, woman?" he said with a teasing lilt in his voice.

"That I am. Now are you going to do as you're told, or do I need to tell your ma on you?"

He stood then, and I felt a tiny prickle of apprehension. But he merely pulled my chair out and gestured for me to sit. I sat.

"Just bein' a gentleman, waitin' on you," he said. "Now button up your lip and tuck in yourself."

I obeyed, happily this time.

He nodded, and we ate in comfortable silence. When he was done eating, he pushed himself away from the table. "Hannah okay?" he asked.

"Oh, she's fine, just dozing off," I replied.

Crossing his arms, he gave me a sober look. "And how's little Ruth?"

I sighed and smiled sadly. Hearing him call me little Ruth, I felt I wanted to cry, or climb into bed and not get up again for a good long while. I remembered his hands on me earlier that day, and how he'd brought me to ecstasy in this very cabin. I remembered his stern look in the barn and how he'd waited for me until I woke up. I wanted more of him.

Ever so slowly, he unfolded his arms and opened them up to me.

"Come here, honey."

I felt the comfort in his voice, as warm and sweet as the name he called me, and I trembled as I crossed over to him. When I stood in front of him, he tugged me onto his lap.

I'd never sat on a man's lap before. The only men I'd ever known well were my pa and my husband, and neither had ever cared for me. I feared I would feel like a child sitting upon Samuel's knee. But I was wrong. It felt quite nice, and for once I was grateful for my diminutive stature. I liked being held in his strong arms, or sitting upon his lap. His arms encircled me, and my head fell to his chest.

"You need to get home," I murmured, not that I had any desire to let him go, but because it felt the right thing to do.

"You let me worry about that," he said. His voice was thick and husky, and it was then I noted his arousal. I could feel him harden beneath me. I closed my eyes. It pleased me, knowing I could do that to him, to be wanted and not simply taken.

He stood, carrying me into my bedroom, laying me gently on the bed. His mouth came to mine and he kissed me, hard and with purpose. As his lips met mine, I felt my body yearning for his. I wanted him to possess me, own every inch of my skin. I wanted to be closer to him, in every possible way. I needed him. But he pulled away from me, leaning up on one elbow.

"I do need to get going home now, honey," he said

softly.

I sighed. I knew he did. Night was falling, and he had chores to do at his own place, too. "Will you come back to me?" I whispered.

"I'll be here first thing in the mornin'," he promised. He stood, giving my fingers one final goodnight kiss.

I knew then that I wanted the day to come that he did not have to go home.

• • • • • • •

I woke up the next day as ornery as a hungry she-bear. I'd had bad dreams, plagued with Hannah's screams, her falling, and my inability to help her. Not being able to protect her fully had been a reality for a good long while.

When I sat up in bed, I had to remind myself that this wasn't what it once was. Yesterday was only a minor setback. Things were different now. Now, I didn't have an abusive husband who would barge into the room in the middle of the night and foist himself upon me. I didn't have to worry about him attacking us when he'd return home from his days of drinking. Now, it was just the two of us.

It was a bit cool outside, so I took my shawl and wrapped it around my shoulders, heading out for a brisk walk. I wanted to pull up weeds by their roots and tear them with my bare hands, or take the axe and swing it hard, splintering the wood in our yard into tiny pieces. I wanted to pound my fists on bread dough, or churn butter until perspiration dripped down my face. The anger inside me needed release.

I tried to focus on the twitter of the sparrows and the sound of little rabbit feet in the woods, to listen to the distant murmur of the creek, and to allow the quiet of the morning soothe me. When I finally reached the water's edge, I plunged my hands into the cool depths. I felt the chill straight through to my bones, and it was welcome. Cupping water into my hands, I lifted it to my mouth, drinking deeply, and when I was done, I ran my cooled hands along my face and neck. I closed my eyes and sighed. It felt nice, being alone here, the brisk water soothing my troubled mind and heart.

I heard the snapping of twigs before I saw him, his tall profile beneath the shadows of the birches overhead causing my heart to flutter. He was so handsome. And I loved him.

The sudden realization terrified me. My fear made me even angrier.

"Little Ruth, I thought you agreed not to come here alone?" he chided.

"I did," I said, getting to my feet. "*Yesterday.* Today is a new day."

He stood still and blinked, his arms slowly crossing over his chest. He leaned his form against a tall oak, and placed one foot up against the bark. He frowned. I could barely see his eyes beneath the brim of his hat, but I could see his mouth. His lips thinned as he frowned.

"I've not managed to convince you to stay safe then, have I?"

Ignoring the question, feeling the implied threat go straight between my legs, I dipped my bucket, filling it with the cool, fresh water. I rose to my feet and turned my back to him, walking home, as I muttered loud enough for him to hear, "And I've not yet convinced you that I like to be left alone."

I could hear him behind me, his footsteps gaining on me with every crack and snap of the twigs beneath his heavy boots. He was coming at a rapid pace, and I wondered if that meant he was angry. My heartbeat accelerated. I quickened my pace, but I was carrying a heavy bucket of water, and his legs were far longer than mine.

"Give me that bucket," he ordered.

"I can hold it myself," I said from behind clenched teeth, and before I knew what was happening, his hands were on mine, and the bucket was taken from me. He placed it on the ground. He snatched my wrist in his own, spun me around, and landed one hard, solid swat to my skirt-clad bottom.

"Young lady, I've had quite enough."

I gasped, my hands flying to my backside. I was too shocked to be angry, finally lifting my eyes to his. His unapologetic act of dominance awakened in me something elusive but undeniable. I liked him being in charge. I could see his shadowed eyes now that he was standing in front of me. He merely grabbed the bucket in one hand and my hand in the other. I tried to pull my hand away but he held tight.

"How dare you—"

He looked down on me, interrupting me. His eyes flashed, and I couldn't remember seeing him so angry. "No, Ruth. How dare *you*? I've done everything I could to keep you safe, watchin' over you when Leroy was on the loose and we feared for your safety. Buildin' you that solid house sturdy enough to keep out predators. And now I come to check in on you, and I'm met with outright defiance?"

We were walking quickly back to the barn, and I couldn't see his eyes. I merely continued to glare ahead of me as he tugged me along by the hand.

"I can take care of *myself*," I said. "I don't need your help!"

We'd reached the barn. He placed the bucket of water down, and now that he had two free hands, he pulled me into him. One hand went to my jaw, gently but firmly holding my face and staring me in the eyes.

"Woman, you'd try the patience of a saint," he said.

"You're not a saint," I spat out, and I was about to reply with another scathing retort, when he leaned in and his lips met mine. His hand still on my jaw, the other went to the small of my back, drawing me closer to him. I was awash with the scent of coffee and hay and tobacco. I could feel not only his hand on my jaw and back, but with his flank pulled up against me, his hardness right against my stomach. His mouth tasted like mint, and as his tongue flicked into my mouth, another lick of arousal heated my core. He was backing me up, back against the wall, and I couldn't stop him if I wanted to. But I did not want to.

A need rose in me, the need to feel him, stronger and harder than he was now, not just his lips but all of him. I needed him to take me as I was, to help me forget my anger and my hurt, and to drive my frustrations out of me.

He released my jaw, steered me away from the wall and lowered me to the ground, the soft hay prickling my back, his arms still cradling me as he continued to kiss me. His hand smoothed over my skirts. My hips rose at his touch. I kissed him fiercely, almost angrily, wanting him not to just kiss me but to *take* me. I wanted to be claimed, owned, possessed, every bit of me his.

His hand hiked up my skirt and roved over my undergarments, pushing past the layers until he found my sensitive parts. He groped as my hips jerked upward. He'd brought me to ecstasy once, and now here, in this heated moment with his lips plundering my mouth, I felt my need building again. When he pulled his hand away, I whimpered into his mouth.

He lifted his mouth to my ear. "Am I too rough with you?"

"No," I moaned. "*No.* I need you rougher and stronger. I need to feel you," I said.

One hand went to my hair that had fallen loose from the knot I typically wore, and his fingers glided through the mass of it. I felt his grip tighten as he pulled my head back, lifting my mouth to his. He moved his torso against mine, grinding into me, as I felt the tug in my scalp tingle with his lips locked on mine. I moaned. My need for him was rising, the need to be possessed by him nearly painful.

"Please, Samuel," I whispered. "Take me."

"No, not here, Ruth," he whispered back. "Not like this." And I knew then that he didn't want to take me on the floor of the barn, in the heat of the moment, but rather when we had privacy, and could ease our way into things.

I moaned when he said no. I didn't want him to say no.

How could I convince him otherwise?

He pulled up from me then and looked in my eyes. "Best be gettin' back in that house, now, woman," he said. He was trying to do the right thing, but I could tell that it was killing him to pull himself away. The knowledge pleased me.

"Stay with me, Samuel," I whispered. He looked at me curiously for a moment.

"Stay with you?" he whispered back, brow furrowed.

"At the cabin," I explained, my chest heaving with want and unfulfilled need. "Come in with me and let's have breakfast. Hannah will be glad to see you."

He pushed himself to his feet and took my hand. "All right, then. I ain't goin' to town for a bit longer yet. I can breakfast with you, if you have enough."

My pride felt the stabbing accusation. I lifted my chin. "Of course we have enough," I said. "Won't you come?" The unasked questions in my mind plagued me.

Do you want me? Do you feel as I do? If this is wrong, must we stop?

His voice was firm, yet gentle. "Now, Ruth, I'm not implyin' you can't provide for Hannah or any other such thing," he asked. "You Watson girls are hard workers. It's just that sometimes we have only enough cooked for one meal. I'm just checkin' to see if my eatin' with you will take away from what you or Hannah needs."

My heart fluttered, and I wasn't sure if it was from his firm tone, or his gentle concern for our well-being. I nodded. "We have plenty, Samuel," I whispered, chastened. When would I learn to curb my temper?

He tugged me by the hand toward the house, snatching up the water bucket on the way. There were so many questions I wanted to ask him, so many uncertainties I wanted laid to rest, and my frustration with everything— him, my flaming arousal, and my situation—was making me angrier than ever.

When we arrived at the house, Hannah was awake and had gotten herself ready. I was impressed she'd taken care of herself so well even injured, but that was my girl.

"Mornin', Mr. Stanley," she said politely, and he nodded to her.

"How're those little birds of yours farin'?" Samuel asked. She smiled, chattering away about how she'd already gotten them grubs and water, and they were making a veritable ruckus in her room.

I watched the two of them wistfully. I hated that my daughter never had the love and attention of a father. Now, seeing Samuel with Hannah made my heart yearn to have my daughter cared for in ways I couldn't provide.

Samuel had removed his hat and hung it on a peg by the door, his longish, sandy-brown hair rugged and handsome. He sat up straight in the chair, and I watched his strong hands bringing the steaming mug of coffee to his lips. I remembered what it felt like to have those lips on me, and I shifted uncomfortably in front of the stove. I wanted to be alone with him, to pick up where we'd left off. I started when a knock came on the door.

"Who is it?" I said as Hannah rose.

"It's Pearl!" came the familiar voice. I nodded to Hannah, who opened the door quickly. Pearl had a basket on her arm, and her pretty eyes were shining.

"Morning! Ruth, look," she said excitedly, stepping into the cabin while Hannah shut the door behind her. She lifted the small towel that covered her basket. Inside was a pile of squeaky little chicks, fluffy balls of buttery feathers. Hannah squealed.

"We have too many," Pearl said, "and Aaron says I need to give you some because I'll have my own little chickie to tend to before long."

I smiled. Aaron and Pearl were very good at framing their generosities to allow for my pride to step aside and accept what they gave me.

"Oh, Ma!" Hannah said, her uninjured arm reaching out as one little finger gently stroked the soft feathers of a little chick. "They're so cute!"

I smiled as Samuel tucked into his eggs and toast. "Adorable," he muttered. "They'll make lovely stewed chicken. Maybe even a plump roaster in there. I love me some roast chicken and gravy."

Hannah's jaw dropped in horror, her eyes widened, and I stifled a giggle.

Pearl frowned at him. "Just like your brother," she muttered. "Unapologetic about preying on the innocent!"

Samuel shrugged and shot her a wicked grin. "Life on the prairie, ladies." He'd eaten his three slices of toast and just as many eggs in the time it took me to dish up Hannah's breakfast.

"You go on and eat your breakfast, Hannah. It's time you be getting to school." I paused. "Or maybe you should stay home today."

Samuel took a sip out of his own mug before he spoke. "Did Dr. Gentry say she needed to be home?" he asked.

I blinked in surprise. "Well, no," I said. "But she's injured."

He shrugged and sat back, taking another pull from the mug. "Her right hand ain't injured. I see no need for her to stay home."

I frowned. I felt as if he was overstepping his bounds, and I didn't like it. "But I'm her ma, Samuel," I said, turning back to the stove.

"Now, little Ruth—" Samuel began, but I interrupted him.

"I thank you for your help, Samuel, but I can see to the caring of my own daughter."

I saw Pearl sit up in the chair next to Samuel. Samuel didn't move. He looked at me placidly, but when he spoke, his voice had deepened. "School's almost out for the year," he said. "They'll be doin' exams soon, and she's made it all the way to the brink of the next class. I've seen her studyin' with Matthew, and heard tell in town that she's advancin' rapidly. It'd be a mistake to let her stay home today, when all's she needs to do is be careful she don't hurt her arm."

His jaw clenched.

"Samuel's right," Pearl said.

My temper surged. I hated that they knew things I didn't. Why did *I* not know she was ready to advance? I didn't like being made out to be the bad mother. I'd given my all to be a good mother. Now the two of them were piling hot coals on me, reminding me of how I'd failed. I turned to the stove and began cleaning up. I didn't trust myself to speak for a minute.

Hannah broke the silence. "Ma, I'd rather go to school," she said. "Is Matthew coming by?" she asked Samuel.

Pearl answered. "Oh, he's already in the barn doin' your chores," she said. "He came when I did."

I quickly packed Hannah's lunch pail and helped her get out the door, just as Matthew came in. He was scowling when he came to the door. "Chores done," he said. "And y'all need to sister that beam in your barn afore it comes fallin' down. But I ain't doin' it, seein' as I've already done enough chores for—" He stopped suddenly when he realized Samuel was sitting at the table beside Pearl.

"Mornin', Matthew. Want to repeat that?" Samuel asked sternly.

Matthew scowled, kicking at the floor. "Beam in the barn needs sisterin'," he said. Sistering would entail nailing a stronger, sturdier beam to the one already there.

Samuel nodded. "You come here after school, and the two of us will get that done." Samuel turned to Matthew and Hannah. "You two go on and skedaddle," he said, flicking his fingers to the door. "And Matthew, you mind what I say."

After the two children left, I turned back to Pearl and Samuel, and both of them were looking at me strangely. Samuel's look was calculating, but Pearl's curious. Samuel took his cup and plate and handed them to me, walking to the door and retrieving his hat. He placed it upon his head and turned to me.

"I'll see you this afternoon," he said. "I'm sisterin' that

beam, and I'd better not come back and find you've touched it. You hear?" he asked, pointing one bossy finger in my direction, before he opened the door, nestling the basket of little chicks against him as he let himself out. "I'll take these chicks to your barn. You latch the door behind me," he called over his shoulder.

The door shut. I slammed it, latched it shut, and felt Pearl come right up behind me.

"Ruth, what has gotten *into* you?" she asked. She was standing now, her arms across her chest, glaring at me. "Do you have any idea how hard he works for you? He does his chores and then comes on over here and does yours for you. Do you even know what he does around here when you're busy, or out? Who do you think mended the fence when your cow leapt it? Who do think mended the barn door when you were busy with the maple boiling at Ma's? Do you think little elves come in the middle of the night and do all your work?"

Hot fury licked at my chest. "I did not tell him to do *any* of those things!" I shouted. "I'm fully capable of handling them myself! I did not ask for help, and he had no right coming on my property while I was gone!" I wanted to go and fetch him, and shake some sense into him.

Pearl took a step closer to me. "How dare *you*!" she said. "He bends over backwards to help you and for what? No thanks, and a smart mouth, that's what!"

I don't know what came over me then. Pearl was my very best friend in the world. I adored her. But it was as if some strange creature had come over me and the horrible knot in my chest overtook me. My hand shot out and before I knew what I was doing, I'd slapped her straight across her cheek. She screamed and covered her cheek with her hand, her eyes registering anger and shock. I was overcome with horror the second my hand struck her face, and my own hands covered my mouth.

"Oh, Pearl!" I said, overcome with emotion and regret. "I… I didn't mean to. I'm so sorry! Oh, Pearl!" Tears blurred my vision as I led her to my rocker by the fire.

"I shouldn't have shouted at you," she whispered, her eyes shut tight. Her hands dropped to her lap and I could see the telltale red marks of my handprint on her cheek. I touched her gingerly as I wept.

"I'm so sorry," I moaned. "Oh, I'm so sorry. I never meant to hurt you. And you, with child." I dropped to my knees in front of her and stroked the handprint on her cheek.

"I'm all right, Ruth. You didn't mean to," she said softly. The fact that she wasn't angry with me somehow made me feel worse. I wanted her to smack me back, as I deserved some sort of retaliation for what I'd done. "But Ruth, we must do something about this. If Aaron finds out… ohhh," she whispered, covering her face with her hands. Aaron was so fiercely protective. "He wouldn't let me see you anymore," she whispered, her own tears flowing now. "He'd not allow me to visit if he knew you struck me."

I covered my face with my hands and wept. What had I done? What could be done to fix this?

A knock came at the door, and before I could answer, it swung open. Samuel stepped in, removing his hat. "Now, Ruth, I went to check out the beam Matthew mentioned, and I—" He paused as he became aware of the scene in front of him, me kneeling in front of Pearl, her hands up to the pink handprint on her cheek, both of us in tears. "What in tarnation is goin' on in here?"

He listened as I blubbered my story to him. "And he'll never let me see her again," I wailed at the end.

He stood with his feet planted apart, his arms across his chest, working his jaw before he spoke. "You all right, Pearl?" he asked.

She nodded. "I don't even feel it anymore," she said. I wondered if she was lying, but I still threw my arms around her and hugged her.

Samuel nodded. "All right. Looks like this is a case of you oversteppin' your place, and little Ruth losin' her temper." He paused, and his voice deepened. "You both ought to be ashamed of yourselves," he chided. I had no response. He was right.

He shook his head. "Pearl, you get on home and tend to that cheek," he said. "Ma always used a cool cloth if we'd gotten into a fight at school. You rest up. I'll tend to Ruth, and I'll also tend to Aaron tonight. All right?"

Pearl stood, wiping her eyes and sniffling. I stood with her and we embraced.

"I'm so sorry," I whispered in her ear. "Please, won't you forgive me?"

"Oh, honey, of course I do," she whispered back. "It was my own fault for not mindin' my own business. Aaron would put me over his knee for that alone," she said with a laugh, kissing my cheek, and heading to the door.

He'd put her over his knee?

She left, and Samuel shut the door behind her. He turned slowly to face me, his hands going to his hips. "And what am I goin' to do with *you*, young lady?" he asked sternly. This time, I had no smart answer. I could not bring myself to respond. I hung my head in shame as he stalked over to me. One finger placed under my chin, he lifted my face while I tried to blink back the tears that would not stop.

"I don't know," I whispered, my voice shaking as I cried. "I feel awful. Just awful." The anger from earlier, the feeling of helplessness, and the weight that saddled my shoulders seemed insurmountable. I wanted to climb into bed and pull the quilt over my head. I wanted to never get out of that bed again. I deserved to be punished for such a wicked act against my closest friend, and the guilt I felt was consuming me. I covered my face with my hands, tears seeping through my fingers. "She's so good to me," I choked, as the tears flowed. "She's with child, and I struck her. What a wicked, wicked thing. I feel so guilty, Samuel," I said to him. "I ought to be whipped for such a thing."

His arms came around me then, and he pulled me into his chest. One large hand stroked my hair as he held me. "I wouldn't say whipped," he said, and his voice was softer than I expected. "But little Ruth, I've long since thought that my hand across your backside would do you a world of good."

I sniffled onto his chest as he held me. Just now, Pearl had told me Aaron would've taken her across his knee. She said it with a laugh, even. Would I feel better if he spanked me?

He'd told me he wouldn't raise a hand to me, because of my past.

But would he if I *asked*? I pulled back from him.

"Samuel?"

He nodded, smoothing the dampened hair back from my forehead.

"Would you... spank me if I told you that I knew I deserved it? And I wouldn't... be angry with you? I feel guilty," I said. "I ought to be spanked."

His eyes focused on mine a minute. He was contemplating. He finally spoke after what seemed a very long time.

"You want me to spank you?"

I closed my eyes and nodded. I couldn't look at him.

"Fair enough," he said.

I swallowed, fear racing across my chest and a surprising jolt of arousal at his stern but calm demeanor. "Now?" I whispered.

He released me, pulled a chair from the table, placed it in the center of the room, and sat heavily, his large legs spread apart. I looked at his lap and wondered what it would feel like to lie across his knees like a naughty child. He would not make me. He would not forcefully pull me across his lap.

Samuel patted his knee. "Come now, little Ruth," he said softly. "Come and lay yourself across my knee."

He would not force me.

I would have to do it myself.

CHAPTER FOUR: THE SPANKING

Samuel was waiting. As I looked at him sitting in the chair, his brows furrowed and gaze uncompromising, my sex pulsed with need. I shifted uncomfortably.

He patted his lap again.

Ever so slowly, I dragged my feet toward him. What was I doing? Why had I asked him to punish me?

When I reached him, he gently took one of my small hands in his larger one. His voice was low and husky. "You need this, honey," he whispered. My throat clogged once again from unshed tears, from both the sweet words and the knowledge that he was going to help me. He was right. I needed him to take control.

Slowly, ever so slowly, one silent tear rolling down my cheek, I lowered myself over his lap. I felt his strong thighs beneath me as the breath whooshed out of me. My feet came straight off the floor as my entire torso spread straight across his lap. He placed one firm hand onto my the small of my back, as the other slowly lifted my skirts. I held my breath. I squeezed my eyes shut. What would it feel like? How badly would it hurt?

"Young lady, why do I have you across my lap like a naughty little girl?" he asked. My heart thundered in my chest so that I could hardly stand it. This time, hearing *young lady* felt different. Fitting.

I swallowed. "I... lost my temper," I whispered. "I slapped Pearl." As the words came, so did my tears, flowing more freely now as I said out loud how horribly I'd treated my friend. I felt a breath of air as he finished lifting my skirts, the warmth of his palm on the thin cotton of my undergarments. I'd been bared to him before, but this was somehow more embarrassing and I wasn't even bared. I felt his hand raise, then the first hard smack of his palm fell across my backside. It hurt more than I'd expected it to, and I was both humbled by the correction and astounded he'd actually spanked me that hard. The sound of the slap resonated in the cabin. I gasped, but stayed over his lap. I'd asked him to spank me. He was too tall for me to touch the floor in front of me, so I gingerly grasped his legs. I would take my punishment.

Another hard swat fell, then another. He paused several seconds between each punishing swat. I felt the searing pain of his palm across my skin, but it felt different from the times I'd been hurt before. This was not a beating. This was not belittling. I had consented. This was somehow cleansing, like a steaming hot bath, washing me of the grime and dirt of the day. Stroke upon stroke of his palm fell, and with each smack of his hand, I felt a bit of what I'd been holding onto strip away from me.

His voice was low and stern. "You've had this comin' for a good long while, little Ruth." The swats fell slowly, the bite of his palm on my bottom inexplicably both stinging yet welcome. I wanted him to stop, and I wanted him not to. It hurt, but it wasn't unbearable. I could focus on nothing but the burn of his palm on my backside.

I focused on each lift and fall of his hand. Every flash of pain removed one more layer of hurt. Each smack made the pain inside me more bearable. My mind no longer swirled in torment, but rather surrendered to him.

Now I cried, tears flowing freely as the knot in my chest

dissolved. I sniffled, running a hand across my eyes. He paused for a second, one warm hand still positioned on my lower back, before he administered the hardest swat he'd given me yet.

My eyes were closed, tears coursing down my cheeks, as he pulled me to standing before drawing me to his chest. I was dimly aware of his hands wrapping around my legs and lifting me, that we were moving, and he was carrying me. My hands were around his neck and my face upon his chest as I cried. No one had ever soothed me like this before, with a soft "*shhh*." As he walked to the bed, I felt like it was not just me he carried, but my hurt. I no longer felt guilt. I simply felt that the sadness in my chest had been released. I'd submitted to him. I'd been laid bare.

He laid on the bed and pulled me up on his chest. After a time, my tears slowed. I closed my swollen eyes, and I held him so tightly he chuckled. My arms wrapped around him as if I were a drowning woman and he was my savior. I hiccupped, eyes still shut tight.

"Hold me tight," I whispered. It was not a command but a plea.

Strong, muscular arms embraced me and squeezed. I was completely enveloped by him. We lay there in silence, my hitched breathing intermingling with his own slow breaths. And as I lay there, I felt the calm after the storm descend. Finally, I lifted my face to his. I'd been stripped of my pride and anger. With a simple spanking over his knee, he'd broken down the barrier I'd spent a lifetime building. I was no longer the proud woman who held others at a distance. He'd seen me at my most vulnerable and he hadn't taken advantage of me, mocked me, or hurt me.

He'd given me the spanking fitting a naughty child for my naughty behavior, and in so doing unearthed the woman who loved him.

He placed a finger under my chin, his lips coming to my forehead and gracing me with a tender kiss.

I was so close to him then, I felt his deep voice vibrate

over my body. "Feel better, honey?" he said.

I nodded and sniffled.

He smiled. "Wasn't sure how you'd feel after I gave you a lickin'. And I can't say I haven't wanted to do that for a good long while."

I laughed through my tears. It was a relief, laughing like this, as he held me. "Well," I said. "If I'm honest, I can't say I haven't deserved it for a good long while." I sighed as I remembered why he'd punished me. "Samuel?"

"Yes, honey."

I squeezed my eyes tight. I couldn't trust myself to speak above a whisper. "Will Aaron keep Pearl from me? Will I be allowed to see her again?"

He snorted. "Pearl needs a good spankin' herself for how she treated you," he said. "Don't you trouble yourself with that now. I'll talk to Aaron tonight, and it'll be fine."

I wasn't so sure, but I was in no position to argue. I nodded meekly.

He chuckled again.

"What is it?" I asked.

He shrugged, his eyes twinkling. "Oh, it's just that I like having meek little Ruth in my arms," he said. "And if I'd known all it'd take was a spanking to break through to you, I'd have tanned your hide a long time ago."

I sniffed. "I'd have liked to see you try," I grumbled.

He chuckled, but lifted my chin with his finger again. "Now, Ruth," he said. "You behave yourself."

He seemed stronger and sterner, and the memory of just moments before being laid across his lap caused a pulse of excitement in my chest, which only continued to rise as he went on.

"I'm tellin' you this, young lady. I spanked you once, and it was what you needed. This time, I asked you to grant me that permission. And you did. Now I know you won't feel harmed like you did before, when you were mistreated. I'm holding my little Ruth in my arms, after gettin' her little bottom spanked, as meek and calm as a well-fed kitten. I'll expect you to behave yourself goin' forward. If you don't, I'll not hesitate to bring you straight across my knee again."

I closed my eyes, overcome with my need for him, the words causing me to shift and squeeze my thighs together. At the very same time, I felt relieved. He wouldn't let me carry on like a shrew, and he'd be here to pick up the pieces when I faltered.

"I understand," I said, wanting to thank him but still feeling self-conscious about it.

His eyes darkened. "And if you ever pull some of the stunts you've pulled this week, the next time I spank you, I'll spank your bare bottom, little lady."

"Well, now, let's not get carried away," I responded, though my heart thundered in my chest and I smiled at him. His lips quirked up. He placed his hands under my arms and heaved me further up his chest.

His lips met mine. I closed my eyes. I was in the presence of a stern, uncompromising man, so strong and kind, bearing the mark of his hand upon my skin. Now I wanted to be owned by him in every possible way. I wanted to be claimed, and mastered, filled with nothing but him. His hands went to my face and he held me as our kiss deepened, hot as blazes, flaming my need for him. My thighs shifted beneath my skirts, and I remembered his hand between my legs. I needed more of him.

As we kissed, his hands made their way to the back of my dress. It was simply sewn, with few buttons. He gathered up my skirts as he sat up, lifting me and turning so that now I lay flat on my back and he above me. It was then I noticed his arousal tented in his trousers. It pleased me.

His hands spanned my waist. I needed *more.*

I placed my hands flat on his chest, feeling the strength beneath his shirt.

What happened next was a blur of passion and heat, as I fiddled with my layers of clothing and he unbuttoned his shirt. We both knew what we needed. No words were necessary. When I was bared to him and he to me, he lowered himself back down to me again. The feel of his naked skin against mine flared my arousal again. I could still feel the sting in my backside against the quilt, the throbbing need for him, and his hardened length between my legs as he kissed me. I longed to feel him inside me.

His tanned, muscled arms encircled me. I felt all of Samuel, his breath on my skin, his warmth against me, as he gently nudged my knees apart.

"Are you ready, little Ruth?" he whispered. "Are you sure?"

"Don't stop now," I breathed. "Please don't stop now. I need you."

He closed his eyes and dropped his head to my chest as he thrust into me. I felt at once consumed and needier, my hips rising to meet him. I loved the feel of my burning skin on the blanket and being overpowered. My breath came in gasps and I was already nearing ecstasy. It was only moments after he began that I panted, toppling over the edge, a thrill running from my chest down to my thighs and all the way to my toes, my entire body humming, and he was right there behind me. It felt so right, so natural.

But as we lay there in the stillness, holding one another in the aftershock of a spanking followed by lovemaking, the haze began to lift.

What had we done?

• • • • • •

How could things be normal now? After I'd been taken across Samuel's knee and *spanked*? When I'd cried in his arms, then lain on the bed and been taken by him?

Now he needed to get to his work, and me to mine. As I mopped my floor, kneaded my bread, and mended Hannah's stockings, I felt the sting on my bottom, the ache between my legs, and I kept finding myself staring, marveling at what had transpired. I wasn't sure if I was ready for things to be different between us. Even in misery, there's comfort in familiarity.

When Hannah returned from school, Matthew joined her. I watched from the window in the kitchen. Hannah was chattering animatedly to Matthew, who held his books and lunch pail in one hand and her books and lunch pail in another. I wondered, for a moment, what Samuel was like when he was Matthew's age. Had he always been somewhat sober, steadfast, and dependable? I watched as the two walked to the barn, Hannah's braids gleaming in the sunlight and Rascal, Matthew's little dog, following beside them. We had no meat again, and I was eager to go back to a simple meal of beans, cornbread, and vegetables. I anticipated Matthew and Samuel staying for supper, as I wasn't sure how long it would take for them to fix the beam in the barn.

I felt my stomach flutter in anticipation when I realized Samuel would return soon. What happened after two friends became lovers?

What we had done was shameful, sinful some might even say.

But my only regret was that we'd waited so long.

I thrummed the table with the butt of my knife, the greens now prepared for supper. My stew simmered and bubbled on the stove as I placed my bread in the oven. Moments later, the cabin warmed with the comforting smell of bread baking.

"Smells delicious in here," I heard Samuel's voice rumble. I spun around to look at the doorway, but the door was shut fast. I looked wildly about me, hearing naught but a manly chuckle. I knew that voice. Finally, after several moments' frantic search, I saw Samuel leaning in the tiny window in the cabin.

I wagged my finger. "You're enough to scare a woman out of her wits!" I chided, which elicited another chuckle from him. He stepped away from the window, and I hoped he was coming to the door. I felt bereft already.

A moment later, I heard a knock at the door. I fairly skipped. I hadn't felt this light and airy since I was a child, and even then I couldn't recall being so joyful. I unlatched the door, and he entered, carrying a basket of eggs.

"I'd like to kiss you, but it seems you've got your hands full," I murmured.

He grinned. "You need my hands free before you can kiss me?"

My cheeks flushed at his comment, the sudden recollection of what his hands had done to me while he kissed me making my legs grow weak. He seemed to remember at the same time as I did, his eyes heating and the grin widening.

"Well, take this basket and I'll kiss you proper."

I stepped closer to him, obediently taking the basket. His hand shot out, grasped my elbow, and tugged. I squealed as he held me close and his lips met mine once again. Though the kiss was brief, his hands lingered at my waist.

This wouldn't do. Oh, this would not do one bit. I was finding him irresistible and *I could not find him irresistible.*

I pulled away.

"How are your birds?" he asked, traipsing to Hannah's room. "Land's sake, Ruth, it smells good in here." He scrubbed a hand over his brow as he peeked in to see how the baby songbirds were doing.

He looked tired. I wanted to invite him to sit by me, while I rubbed his back and fetched him a cool drink. I wanted to sit upon his lap and run my hands through the rugged locks of hair. I felt more relaxed than I had in years, more rested than I had in even longer.

But as the desires swept over me to do these things, I could not, *would* not look at him. No. My independence had come at a price so dear, I could not relinquish it so easily to any man. Though my heart yearned to be led by him, I owed allegiance to myself above any other. I could not betray my hard-won freedom.

I had a job to do.

"Oh, they're doing fine," I said, stirring the stew on the stove. They truly were. Matthew and Hannah had gotten some worms for them the evening before, and they were growing bigger by the minute. In another week or two, it would be time to let them go.

He came out of Hannah's room. "Goin' to see to that beam in your barn," he said.

"I'll join you," I said, placing the lid back on the stew. "You may need an extra set of hands to help you."

He turned to face me. "Tryin' that angle again, are you?" he asked, his eyes sobering.

"What angle?" I said irritably. I don't know what came over me then, but I knew I would not be cowed by a look.

"Oh, you know. You have everything you need," he said. "Little Ruth doesn't need help from anyone."

Was he mocking me? I frowned. "I see no need to sister a beam that was placed in a barn not six months ago," I said. "What type of lumber did they use to cause it to need to be replaced so quickly?"

"Could be anythin'," Samuel said with a shrug. "Maybe they didn't realize just how weak the lumber was that they used. Termites have gotten to the wood, or water damage leaked and weakened it."

He walked over to me, and this time as he walked, I stepped backward. His eyes were serious, fixed on me hard, and I gulped as he kept coming. Apparently, having been taken across his knee just that day for a sound spanking had made me look at him quite differently.

He came closer and I moved backward until I stood flat up against the wall, his hands on either side of my hips as he spoke to me. "Are you causin' trouble again, little Ruth? I thought you learned your lesson."

I swallowed, not sure how to respond.

"Already, the memory of my hand on your backside has faded?"

My pulse raced and my mouth went dry. "Noooo," I whispered, my legs weak with both fear and desire.

Damn my body that *would* betray me.

His mouth came to my ear. "Will you behave then, little

Ruth?"

"Yes, sir," I whispered, nodding. His hand reached to my backside and squeezed just moments before we heard a clatter at the door, and we quickly pulled away.

Whatever had held Samuel at bay before no longer held him. He was now fully prepared to deal with me as he saw fit.

Matthew and Hannah entered moments later.

"Chores done?" Samuel asked Matthew.

"Yes, sir," Matthew said.

"Good," Samuel said, taking his hat off the hook and placing it on his head. "I'm heading out to check on that beam."

Hannah sat at the table with Matthew to do schoolwork. Matthew was scowling as he pulled out his slate and primer. Hannah sat next to him, studying diligently. I stood next to her, my hands in her hair, tidying the messy plait that had gotten loose.

"How does your arm feel?" I asked.

"Oh, it's much better," Hannah said, then her eye caught Matthew's as he looked up from his schoolwork. "I mean, it still hurts, Ma. I don't think I'll be able to do chores for a good long while." Her eyes were twinkling and mischievous.

Matthew's eyes narrowed. "That's not what you said earlier!" he chided. Hannah giggled, so I tugged her braid.

"You leave poor Matthew alone," I said, and Hannah covered her mouth with her hand. They'd sort their chores out fine. I'd be sure Hannah didn't take advantage of the situation, and Samuel would be sure Matthew did as he was told.

Matthew sat next to her with his books, scowling. "Today at the dinner break, I saw Hannah pick up a ball and chuck it," Matthew said. His eyes looked up at me, challenging. "And if she's well enough to throw a ball, I reckon she's well enough to do her own chores again."

I looked reproachfully at Hannah, who merely gave me a sheepish grin.

"I completely agree with you, Matthew," I said. "You no longer have to do Hannah's chores." Hannah's face fell but Matthew grinned. "And I'll talk to your brother about it."

Eager to have an excuse to go see Samuel, I left the cabin and headed to the barn. "Samuel!" I called. I peeked around the edge of the barn. As I turned to look in the direction of the chicken coop, I felt strong arms wrap around me from behind, and I screeched, instinctively elbowing him hard in the ribs.

He groaned, releasing me.

"Don't you do that!" I squealed. "Samuel, you scared the bejesus out of me!"

"What'd I tell you about hittin' me?" he said, his eyes flashing even as he was doubled over.

I bit my cheek to keep from smiling. It wasn't often I bested the man who easily dwarfed me in size. "You said something about hitting you?"

He frowned, crossing his arms on his chest. "Well, let's get that straight now, then," he said. "You'll not hit me or hurt me. I don't take kindly to that, even in jest. You understand me, young lady?"

I took a step toward him and planted my hands on my hips, but I was at a loss for how to respond, for when I opened my mouth to speak, I noticed his arousal tented in his pants. He loved my sass. I decided to push it a bit further.

"Maybe I don't understand," I said, all humor gone now as I scowled at him. "When a mammoth man like you grabs me, I ought to be able to defend myself."

Maybe he loved my sass, but I had pushed too far. Unfolding himself to his full height, he reached a hand out and grabbed my arm. Before I knew what he was doing, he spun me around and landed one hard, uncompromising swat to my backside. I felt my cheeks flame. From behind, his arms wrapped around my chest and his mouth went to my ear.

"Things changed today between me and you," he said

low. He pulled back just a tad, and to my shock, I felt another hard swat land against my skirt-clad bottom. Blood pounded in my ears and my palms grew sweaty as my desire for him was renewed even while I squirmed in embarrassment. "I know how you responded to me today. I know what you need. And honey, I fully plan on giving you what you need." He turned me around to look at him, his hands on my shoulders. "You understand me, little Ruth?"

Did he know what I needed?

How could he know what I did not know myself?

I nodded dumbly. He pulled me closer for a kiss. But even as I submitted to being held by him and kissed, I knew that I could not let this continue.

CHAPTER FIVE: CHASED AND CAUGHT

It amazed me how long I successfully managed to avoid Samuel. It seemed he'd been attached to my side for days, but now, with an effort, I managed to evade him.

I did not go down to the creek to fetch my water; nor did I swing by Ma's while Hannah was in school, to cook, or bake, or mend together. I disliked hastening to the well to fetch my water, but I did not want to risk going to the water alone in the morning, especially as Samuel was so handy with his palm now, and I'd been told not to go. I told myself I wasn't *obedient* to him, but rather it wasn't worth the effort of dealing with him.

Matthew was busy helping Aaron with some jobs on his homestead before the arrival of the new baby, so we saw little of Matthew. I had much to do during the day, and fortunately it seemed my jobs easily took place at the same time as Samuel was working himself.

As I was mending by the fire early one morning, after Hannah had gone to school, I heard a knock come at the door. I leapt to my feet and raced to Hannah's room, where there was no window, peeking out at the window in the main room. It wasn't until I saw his shadow pass the curtain in the main room that I dared creep out again. And it wasn't until I'd picked up my mending again that the realization hit me: I'd been hiding from him. I was not a woman who hid. Even when I had faced a drunken husband who would raise his fist to me, I had never hidden. I had faced him, fought him, and thrown myself at him to protect my daughter.

Then why did I hide now?

Determined not to be pushed to do something I need not do, I got to my feet, placed my mending on the table, and yanked the door to the cabin open. I would face him. If he'd gone back to town, then I would simply walk toward town until we met.

Clouds crept in front of the sun, darkening the sky, and the woods adjacent to where I walked now seemed ominous as elongated shadows danced upon the ground in front of me. I felt a chill creep over my arms, the hairs standing on end. Rubbing my hands briskly over my arms, I continued to walk rapidly, determined to stay on my mission.

The snap of branches immediately behind me made me jump.

"Ruth."

I spun on my heel, the panic I'd felt making me angry. I struck Samuel as hard as I could, my balled fist landing a solid punch to his midsection, causing him to double over. I was so angry with him, I could've smacked him again, but my conscience pricked me when he braced himself on the trunk of a snow white birch, holding one hand out in surrender.

I moved toward him, but his voice thundered at me. "Enough!" he roared. "You raise your hand to me one more time, woman, and you won't sit for a week!"

I froze, painfully aware of the mistake I'd just made. I'd been warned sternly never to raise a hand to him. Still, I felt somewhat justified.

"You scared the living daylights out of me!" I protested. "I thought you were a bandit or savage! How dare you?"

He was still bent over, panting for breath, but his blue

eyes were storm clouds warning of the tempest that lay ahead. "You were walkin' through the woods like Little Red Riding Hood," he said in a short, clipped tone. "With no care for your safety. And I ain't a scholar, little Ruth, but I'm not a fool. I damn well know you were in the cabin hidin' on me. I came behind you just now and didn't mean to scare you."

"That's the most foolish thing I ever heard!" I shouted, not even bothering to modulate my voice. But as he finally regained his breath, unfolding himself to his full length, he towered over me, stern and foreboding. His eyes were thunderous, his nostrils flared. He placed two enormous hands on his hips.

He shook his head. When he spoke it was in a low, warning tone. "Woman," he growled, "I'm fresh out of warnin's for you."

I knew he was coming for me. And I knew when he caught me, I was going to end up belly down and blistered. So I did the smartest thing I could. I turned tail and ran.

I was fast and he was still wheezing, which gave me the decided advantage. I made quick use of my tiny stature, dodging between narrow branches, trying to ignore his growls behind me as nimble limbs snapped back and whipped him. I wasn't sure where I was going or how I would prevent him from getting his hands on me, but I did know I had to try.

I ducked below a weeping willow and around a pine tree, leaping straight over a fallen log and narrowly missing a huge broken branch in front of me. I turned quickly to the left and under an overgrown mass of thistles and ferns, to where I knew a small clearing was hidden. I turned and looking quickly over my shoulder. I breathed a sigh of relief. He was a good distance behind me, hindered by his larger size and my nimble feet. I kept running.

I had run before, my skirts flailing about me, my hairpins jostled from the knot at the base of my neck, with my hair tumbling about me. But those times were not the same as they were now. Now, I ran with my heart tripping within my chest, knowing that when he caught me, and I knew it was only a matter of time, I would be overpowered. That his large, strong body would pin me down, and I'd be helpless. He'd very likely spank me, and I knew I deserved it.

To my right, I saw the dim entrance to a cave, and my desperate mind grasped onto that. I was vaguely familiar with the area, nearby the berry bushes I frequented when the berries were ripe. The cave would be perfect. He was far enough behind me that he wouldn't see me. I dodged to the right, but the minute I came to the entrance of the cave, I froze. The temperature had dropped, and what would be in that cave, anyhow? A bear? Bats? Rats? I knew then I'd rather face Samuel and his wrath than whatever loathsome creatures would be found in the cave.

It only took several seconds for me to decide what to do. But those several seconds were enough. I'd underestimated the speed of a man on a mission.

I spun around, my eyes darting about me to see where to go next, when Samuel stood in front of me. We both froze, staring at each other in the dim light of the forest. Shadows fell across his face from the sun peeking through the branches overhead. Surrounding us, I could hear the familiar twitter, calls, and chirps of the birds, murmur of the creek, and whisper of wind through the leaves. But the loudest sound of all was my own panting and his. I was caught, the prey now at the mercy of my hunter.

His eyes were narrowed, his lips thinned in an implacable line. I wiped my dampened hands on my skirts and met his gaze. He was handsome when he was angry. His blue eyes the color of cornflowers looked darker in the woods. His chest rose and fell rapidly as he sucked in breath. His eyes darted to where I stood and around me, likely trying to see if I could plan another escape route. But there was none. With the cave at my back and a bank of trees on either side of me, the only way out was through him. I was trapped, and he knew it.

He stepped toward me, the crack of the branches beneath his feet making me jump, one firm step after another, until he stood directly in front of me and I had to do what I always did when we stood that close. I craned my neck to look up at him, feeling the stretch along my spine as I lifted wide eyes to his massive form. One enormous hand went to my chin, not rough but not gently, and I felt my face engulfed with his warm, firm touch. I could not look away. His fingers flexed, and my jaw clenched.

He inhaled, still panting, as he spoke. "Young lady," he began, then paused for more breath. His voice was deep, chiding, and I began to tremble as he spoke. "You're in trouble the likes of which you've never known."

I noticed several thin red stripes across his cheeks, where the tree branches had lashed him. He wouldn't have gotten hurt if I hadn't run from him. A stab of remorse hit me, and my eyes misted as I reached one hand to his cheek, tracing a finger along the line.

"I'm sorry," I whispered in a shaky breath. Still holding my chin, he dipped his mouth to my ear.

"Oh, little Ruth," he said. "You will be."

He released my chin and dipped down, both of his hands under my arms as he hoisted me up and straight over his shoulder. I sprawled, helpless, the prey caught with no choice but surrender. I did not fight. I knew I deserved whatever would happen now.

I'd been holding everything on my own now for days. I felt riddled with guilt from having caused him distress and pain. I longed to be close to him again. A small part of me, if I were really honest, *wanted* him to take over.

It was hard to see where we were going, strewn over his back as I was. With the first few steps I noticed a large broken pine, its branch sticking out oddly, but it was the only thing I noticed, as I dared not lift my head too often. Squirming resulted in a firm swat to my backside, so I laid as still as possible. But we were moving out of the forest now, and onto the plain. Still, we walked on.

"If you let me down, I will walk and not run," I said. "I don't want you to hurt yourself, Samuel."

His only response was another sharp swat to my bottom. I fell silent.

We walked on, and I closed my eyes, realizing then that he was heading back to my home. I recognized the area around us now, and knew that soon we'd come to my cabin. I shivered now that my punishment was imminent.

He put me on my feet, then large fingers tightened around my upper arm, marching me forward toward my cabin. He opened the door and tugged me in, shutting the door behind him. With no further ado, he wrapped one large hand around the chair by my table and dragged it to the center of the room, the scrape of the feet echoing in the silence of the cabin. Still holding me, he sat heavily, dragging me forward almost roughly so that I stood between his large knees. His blue eyes bored into mine, his jaw clenched, as he glared at me. I'd hoped the little walk in the woods had calmed his temper. It seemed instead he was angrier now than ever. Both of his hands grasped my waist, and he yanked me even closer to him so that I felt the warmth of his legs straight through my skirts.

"What do you have to say for yourself, young lady?" he asked. I squeezed my eyes shut. I wasn't prepared for the question.

I took a minute to compose myself, before deciding brutal honesty would be best. I opened my eyes. "I've hidden from you for days, yes, I will admit."

Jaw still clenched, he deigned to give me one stout nod. "Go on."

I swallowed, taking a shaky breath before I continued. "I just... was afraid. Not sure what happens next. But I wanted to speak to you, so I followed you. And I never heard you approach. You scared me when you grabbed me like that."

He nodded again and his eyes were still hard. "Why do you think I don't want you in the woods alone? If you don't hear a big, lumbering man like me coming along, how would you hear something that would be a danger to you?"

I cast my eyes down. He had a point.

He jerked my head up to meet him again with his fingers under my chin. "Why did you run?"

Well, that was easy. "Because I knew you'd spank me, and I didn't want a spanking."

Amusement flitted across his features though he remained stern, the barest trace of amusement. "Honey, if I decide you're getting a lickin', you can run, and you can hide, but there's one thing you can count on. I'll lay you across my knee sooner or later, and you'll not only get the lickin' you deserve, you'll answer for the chase. You mark me, woman. Don't you *ever* run from me again."

I cast my eyes down, suddenly repentant for acting like such a child all along.

"Yes, sir," I mumbled. I needed him to fix this.

"Ruth."

I looked back up at him and nodded.

He leaned in, his voice even lower, not much above a harsh whisper. "Remove your clothes."

I gasped. "All of them, sir?" My heart galloped in my chest.

One hand reached out and threaded his fingers through the messy knot of hair before tugging.

"*All of them.*"

· · · · · · ·

My hands shook as I slowly began to undress, layer upon layer of my clothing falling off my shoulders, over my head, down around my ankles. I took my dress and laid it over the back of the chair next to him, followed by my petticoats and stays, and stockings. When I got down to my undergarments, my stomach began to clench. When I was divested of all my clothing, I would be punished. Slowly, with his eyes never leaving me, I pushed my undergarments off until I stood in front of him completely bare.

He crooked a finger at me.

My stomach churning, legs trembling, I choked in a breath. I'd forgotten to breathe.

When I stood in front of him, he grasped my wrist and yanked me even closer so that my naked form pushed against his inner thighs.

"Tell me, Ruth," he said, eyes steely and unwavering, his voice almost harsh. "Tell me why I'm punishin' you."

I swallowed and took a deep breath. "I hid from you. I struck you. And then I ran."

He nodded slowly. "And are those the actions of a full grown woman, young lady?"

I felt ashamed and shook my head. "No, sir."

A finger under my chin brought my eyes back to his. "And what should I do about this, little girl?"

I closed my eyes briefly, inhaling again. I hated having to say it aloud. Opening my eyes, I spoke, my voice just a whisper. "Punish me."

He nodded slowly, and to my relief he didn't make me ask him, or instruct me to lie over his knee. He simply lifted me and placed me belly down exactly where he wanted me. To my surprise, though I still feared the pain of being punished, I also felt something different. As my bare stomach hit his fully clothed thighs, as I felt one firm hand against my lower back, I closed my eyes. In the momentary prelude to my chastisement, what I felt then surprised me.

Relief.

"I'm half tempted to cut a switch or use my belt," he said. "You've done wrong, and I'm none too pleased."

I nodded silently.

"Should I cut a switch or use my belt, little Ruth?"

I was surprised he asked me. I needed him to punish me, and we both knew it. Though those options sounded awful, I said what I truly felt. I needed things to be right again. I needed his arms around me in comfort, not restraint.

"I'll take whatever you think I deserve."

"Good answer," he said, and that was my only warning. I gasped as his large hand descended with a loud smack that echoed in the room.

Another hard swat followed another, and another, until my skin was aflame and the pain nearly unbearable. It hadn't hurt this much before, but this time I was bare, and he was relentless. I tried to take my spanking bravely, but one searing swat across my upper thighs made me cry out. I scissored my legs, consumed by the pain, but he was ready. One heavy leg trapped mine so that now I straddled only one knee, my bare bottom fully exposed and vulnerable. He took my hands and pinned them to my lower back.

"Whatever it takes," he growled. He paused, several seconds between each swat, before resuming with renewed vigor. "To show you I'll not put up with sass, or games, or disrespect." *Swat.* "To show you I *care*." The swat that landed next was the hardest he'd ever given me.

His words along with the pain broke through my stubborn pride, and I began to cry, slowly at first, as he continued to spank me. My skin was on fire, the pain intense. The seconds of pause in between each firm swat of his hand made me hold my breath in anticipation of the inevitable strike of his palm. He did not slow, but spanked me in earnest. Two rapid swats landed on the center of my bottom. I squirmed, wriggling nearly off his lap but he held fast. His hand continued to fall. The spanking would never stop. I would be over his knee forever. I could not stop him any more than I could stop the clock from ticking, or the sun from shining. So I did the only thing I could do. I surrendered.

I lay as still as possible over his knee, doing my best to accept the punishment I knew I deserved. I sank into my state of submission. As the painful torrent continued, there was nothing on my mind now but accepting each rise and fall of his hand. I could hardly bear the pain, but I knew I needed to surrender.

It seemed Samuel knew as well, for it was at this point

he paused, and his hand caressed my flaming hot skin. "My strong, brave girl," he said. "You're a good girl, takin' your punishment. I'm proud of you givin' yourself over to me like this. But I'm not done, little Ruth. Not until you know runnin' from me ain't an option."

His hand was so large he covered my naked skin with one sound swat. I heard the slap of his palm on my bare skin echo in the cabin right as another lick landed, followed by another.

Runnin' from me ain't an option.

I'd run from the only person who'd ever taken the time to chase me.

My body went limp. His hand stilled as I wept. He released my hands and I felt one warm hand rest on my back as the other began to gently massage my hot skin. It was painful to the touch, but the feel of his hand on my skin, intimate and soothing, was welcome.

"Have I made my point, little Ruth?"

I was now crying so hard I couldn't staunch the tears. "You have," I sniffled. "Yes, sir. Samuel, I'm sorry," I wailed. "I'm so sorry."

His large, callused hand continued to caress the surface of my hot, punished bottom.

I hiccupped, swiping a hand across my face, and repeated, "I'm so sorry."

His hand traveled from the top of my bottom down to my thighs, pausing to massage where he'd spanked me. "You're forgiven," he said in a low murmur. "C'mere, honey."

He turned me over on his lap, holding me tightly and cradling me, my head upon his chest. I cried softly, my eyes closed, as he rocked me.

"Shhh, honey," he said softly. "It's forgiven now. All is forgiven, little Ruth, my sweet little Ruth." His tender tone and gentle words made me cry even harder. He'd been stern, and he'd spanked me soundly, my bottom an aching reminder of his love for me. He would not let me run. He would come for me.

I knew that having finally submitting myself to him had done something to the shackles that surrounded me, the shackles of self-doubt and anger. In that moment, I did not think about my past. I did not think about the future. I thought about nothing but being held by him, while my tears flowed freely. I thought about the way his mouth met mine, and how nice it felt, as I ached not just from my punishment, but now with need. I needed his hands on me.

He rose, carrying me, his mouth still upon mine as we kissed. I moaned into his mouth, and he walked faster, laying me gently on the bed, placing kisses upon my damp cheeks, along my temples, down my neck and to my shoulder, his kisses gentle caresses. He pulled me onto his chest and held me as my tears slowed and finally stopped. Running a hand from the top of my head down to my bottom, he gently stroked. Again, his hand traveled the length of my naked body, over the smooth curve of my hip, past the flatness of my stomach, slowly caressing the soft, full swell of my breast. My chest rose as we kissed again, as I thoroughly enjoyed the claiming touch of his rough hand against my bare skin. I whimpered with need as heat lapped at my core. He'd already marked me. Now I wanted more.

His mouth left mine and dipped low, his tongue flicking to my nipple. I closed my eyes, overwhelmed with the sensation. One of his hands dove between my legs and his finger dipped low, plundering my sex. I moaned. The feeling was exquisite as his tongue continued the torturous, heavenly assault on my breast, his fingers knowing just how to probe and stroke. It would not be long before I would be soaring in ecstasy. The sensation of my punished skin in sharp contrast to the building heat between my legs had me gasping, writhing, eyes closed against the brilliance of it all, and I knew now why the French called my mounting pleasure *la petit morte*. My ecstasy was so divine, I'd have died to have my needs met, and I'd have died a happy woman.

Just as I was about to topple over the edge in ecstasy, his

mouth left my breast. I nearly gasped from the shock of it, immediately feeling the loss. But he was not finished. He moved himself down the bed until his mouth was between my legs. His tongue flicked out, circling my sensitive nub. He sucked, then pulled back, the gentlest touch of the tip of his tongue lapping at me. I could hardly stand it. After just a few delicious, perfect strokes of his tongue, I was soaring.

I'd never experienced anything like it. My emotional surrender and the harshness of the spanking had brought all my feelings to the surface. I was primed. My hips jerked as I gave into wave upon wave of pleasure. My heart thundered in my chest, my entire body aflame with brilliant rapture, as I screamed his name, clenching the quilt beneath my hands, the intensity lasting so long I couldn't breathe. As I finally settled back down, he was standing in front of me, stripping himself. He lowered himself down to me, and I opened my legs, so eager to unite with him, eager to have him enter me. My head fell back on the pillow, again overcome with the welcome feeling of bliss as his hardness sought my core, thrusting into me.

He filled my core. Every stroke, every thrust felt exquisite, the burning need to be fully owned by him being met with each jerk of his hips. I knew he was meeting his own ecstasy when his hands fisted, holding me beneath him so hard it was almost fierce, until finally his head dropped to my chest.

But even as I felt that he'd finally claimed what I offered, I wondered how we would be welcomed by everyone. What would his family say if they knew that he and I were intimate without being married? Would they want such a strong, capable, intelligent man to be partnered with a woman who was no better than damaged goods? Would their goodness to me change if they knew what was between us?

The quiet aftermath of our lovemaking was enough for me, for today. But as he held me I couldn't help but feel it was only for a short time. Surely, this couldn't last. I wasn't good enough for him. Not for his family, and certainly not as his future wife. I needed to be held by him for just a moment longer, for I feared that when he released me, I would no longer be his.

• • • • • • •

We lay in bed for some time before Samuel let me up.

"I don't want to leave you," he murmured. "But I have work to do, and your Hannah will be due back any minute. I best be gettin' home. Need to finish my work today, before supper time."

I nodded, covering myself with my blanket. "I've missed everyone," I said. "Especially Ma and Pearl. Is Pearl there today?"

His eyes grew strangely guarded then as he dressed himself. I watched him work his jaw as he buttoned up his shirt. "Might be," he said. "Though Pearl's not been visiting much lately."

I sat up, swinging my legs over the bed. The sting in my bottom was intense, and I winced, but if he noticed, he was unrepentant. "Why hasn't she been around?" I asked as I stepped into my clothing. I pulled my petticoats over my head, and his voice was muffled. My head emerged. "What was that?"

He cleared his throat. "Well, you know her time is coming soon," he said.

I nodded. I did know. She was ready to have her baby within weeks, and it was hard for her to get around. He continued. "Aaron wants her home."

"Well, I understand," I said, pulling on my dress next and smoothing it out. As I covered myself in the layers of fabric, I wondered briefly what it would be like to wake up next to Samuel in the morning. But I shoved the thought away. "I should go on over and visit," I said. "Bring her some food. She must be awfully uncomfortable at this point."

I'd blocked many memories from my mind, but I

remembered giving birth to Hannah vividly, as it was one of the happiest moments of my life. I felt wistful, remembering those early days when I'd nestle my sweet baby to my bosom, rocking her in my chair. Those were the days when I still thought of my husband as a somewhat decent man. He'd prove otherwise.

Samuel's back was toward me now as he bent and reached for his boots. He sat heavily in a chair at the table, still turned away from me. "Well, now, Ruth, I'm not sure that's such a good idea."

I was lacing up my own boots now. "And why is that?"

He cleared his throat. "Aaron won't want you coming by."

I felt the breath whoosh out of me and a sudden chill descend. "He won't?"

Samuel turned to face me and shook his head. "Now, Ruth, don't despair," he said. "I'm sure he'll come around eventually."

My chest constricted and I felt a helpless sort of ache in my gut. "I'm not allowed to be her friend anymore?" I whispered.

Samuel shook his head sadly. "Now, honey, it's not forever. Just for now. He'll change his mind, no doubt. Just give it time, Ruth. He's being unreasonable with the baby about to come."

If I'd had any fight left in me at that point, I'd have cried all over again, but I didn't. I felt defeated. "So he's not allowing her to go to Ma's?" I asked. "He's angry with me for what I did?"

Samuel stroked his beard. "Well, now, at first he was pretty mad. He was bound and determined to have a reckoning with you, but I assured him you'd already been dealt with."

Normally, I'd be embarrassed that Aaron knew Samuel punished me. But now I nodded eagerly, as it was one step closer to having me reunited with Pearl. "But it wasn't enough."

I sat at my table, smoothing out my skirts. The knowledge that I *couldn't* see Pearl was somehow more difficult to take than the knowledge that I simply *hadn't* seen her. The deliberate decision to exclude me from her life stung. But I couldn't really blame Aaron either. I'd sent his wife home with a handprint right across her cheek. I covered my face with my hands. "Oh, when will I learn to curb my temper?" I said.

"Oh, you've already learned how," Samuel said. "You're fully capable of not losing your temper with Hannah, or with those little critters that follow you around. Are you not?"

I nodded slowly. He was right. I never lost my temper with Hannah.

He raised a brow. "Seems to me you only let loose on the ones who can handle you."

I frowned at him, but he had a point. I'd never lost my temper with Matthew, or Hannah, or any of the children. But it was a different circumstance then. They didn't anger me like the others did.

"Seems to me the sooner you learn to control your temper, the better," he said. "But since I'm not always there to teach you, you best learn the only way you have available. And for now, that means you don't get to see Pearl."

Though I felt the sting of his scolding me, I closed my mouth and bit my tongue. I'd not misbehave, not now, after we'd just made love and all was forgiven.

"Maybe so," I said. My eyes dropped, and I couldn't look at him. The sadness from knowing Aaron wouldn't let me talk to Pearl was a heavy weight again. I wanted to help her. She was my only friend who understood me, through and through.

"Well, now," Samuel said, rising. "You don't fret now, little Ruth. You behave like a good girl, and give Aaron and Pearl time." He reached for me, tucking my head against his chest and kissing my forehead. "If you want to go on over to Ma's, I'll be there all afternoon. We can leave now. If

Pearl's there, I'll bring you home. But you don't go alone. You heed me?"

I sighed. "Yes, sir."

As we walked together, his large hand embraced my smaller one. We passed the chapel, which also functioned as the school, and the children were just finishing up their recess. I waved to Hannah, and opened my mouth to tell her to meet me at Ma's after school, but the words froze on my lips. What if I was sent away?

"Come home with Matthew," I said. "And I'll see you tonight." I was hopeful that I would be able to stay at Ma's, but knew that if I were somehow sent away, I knew I could depend on Samuel to see Hannah made it home.

The sun was high in the sky, beating down relentlessly as we made our way to Samuel's home. Everything looked neat as a pin when we arrived. The wood was neatly stacked by the door, and fields were studded with rows of neatly organized crops. To the right, hanging on hooks in the barn right near the loft I'd slept in, I could see a leather saddle in the barn along with Samuel's stout quirt. I shifted as I cast my eyes away, remembering his promise to cut a switch or use his belt before he spanked me. I discreetly passed a hand over my still aching bottom.

"Hello, Ruth!" Ma called from the doorway, her eyes fluttering briefly to our clasped hands. I pulled my hand away from Samuel and waved.

"Wait here a minute," Samuel instructed, before walking ahead of me into the house. He returned a minute later. "Pearl ain't here," he said low.

I felt like a criminal, sending someone ahead of me to check the scene so I knew when to come and plunder. It was mortifying. Thankfully, Ma went back into the house.

"Land's sake," Samuel muttered under his breath.

I looked at him curiously as he pointed a finger at the barn door. Both doors to the barn were wide open.

"Who left those doors open?" I asked.

"Could've been Ma, but likely Matthew," he growled. "I

told that boy to make sure he locked up before he left."

"Well, let's see if anything's awry," I said.

We walked together to the barn so Samuel could check the livestock, and at first everything looked fine. But when we reached the other end where the saddles were hung with care along the wall, Samuel swore under his breath. "Looks like one's missin'," he muttered. "I'm gonna wear that boy out when he gets home."

"Whoever would've taken it?" I asked.

He shook his head. "Not sure. There were locals around who came into town on the latest caravan, and I don't trust 'em one bit." He turned to me with a frown. "It's why you're not allowed out alone, young lady."

I pursed my lips but didn't respond to his bossiness. *Allowed?*

"All right, back to the house," he said. When we reached the door, he grasped the back of my neck and dipped down for a brief kiss. I stood up on my tiptoes, hoping no one had seen. "Come on in now, little Ruth."

I followed him, nodding to Ma and Geraldine as we came in.

Ma rose and came to embrace me. "I've missed you," she said warmly as she pulled me into her bosom. It felt nice, being held like that. Her home smelled like cinnamon and spice, warm bread baking and something delicious cooling on the stove. The room was warm and tidy, the windows and doors open to allow a breeze to come in.

"Well, I was afraid you were doing poorly when we didn't see you for so long," she began. "But it sure looks like you've made up for that and then some. You've got a right flush on your cheeks and you look pretty as a picture. You all right, child?"

"Yes'm," I said. My eyes instinctively shot to Samuel, who was still standing in the doorway. Ma took us both in, her shrewd eyes missing nothing. She tossed an arm over my shoulder and brought me further in. "How's Hannah?"

I nodded. "Hannah's doing well," I said. "Her arm's

healed, and she's off back to school now. She'd done her best to get Matthew to do her chores, but she's well enough now to handle them just fine."

Ma chuckled. "She's a firecracker, that Hannah."

"Oh, that she is."

Ma removed her arm from my shoulders and bustled about the cabin. "You need tea, darlin'?" she asked.

"Yes, please."

"Tea, Geraldine?"

Geraldine nodded.

Geraldine sat by the fire, rocking her little one. While Ma made my tea, I heard Samuel tell Ma about the saddle, their voices rising and falling as they discussed the situation.

I decided to focus on Geraldine. "Hello," I greeted, but she ignored me. Her lovely Mary Jane seemed as if she'd grown since I'd seen her just a few weeks prior, her wisps of blond hair curling around her temples, little button nose and rose-colored mouth fetching and endearing. She was wrapped in a knit blanket, and her little eyes were growing heavy with sleep. I heard the door of the cabin open and close, and I knew Samuel was going back to the barn.

Geraldine spoke in a low whisper. "I know what you're all about, Ruth. And Ma can embrace you and you can do no wrong in her eyes. But in my eyes, I know exactly what it is you're after."

I felt my limbs grow cold, and I wished that Samuel hadn't gone back out to the barn. I lifted my chin. "Yes, I lost my temper. Occasionally, I do," I said. "Though *some* people make it far easier to do." I frowned at her, but I bit my tongue. It would not do to lose my temper now. "What exactly is it that you think I'm after?"

Geraldine frowned. "You want in on the Stanley family. You want to be one of them. So you'll seduce Samuel, and do your very best to get your hands on him. You attack Pearl, and you're doing your best to pull this family apart."

The familiar flash of anger flared in me. I hated her. I hated everything she said, and I hated that I felt, deep down in my bones, that this was how *all* the Stanleys felt about me, only she was the only one who had the nerve to say it.

"You're wrong," I hissed. I heard the whistle of the teakettle, and Ma clattering on the stove. "I lost my temper, and for that I am deeply sorry." I meant every word. "But I would *never* try to hurt this family. I owe you no further explanation."

I turned from her and promptly went to help Ma with the tea. My heart hammered in my chest, and my palms were damp. How dare she make such an accusation? I'd done nothing to deserve it, and it hurt far more than I would have thought. I stirred milk and sugar in my tea, and sank gratefully in a chair. How long had it been since I'd sat with a cup of hot tea? I'd done nothing but work the past few weeks.

"Feeling all right, Ruth?" Ma asked. I blinked, placing my teacup gingerly on the table.

"I'm fine," I said, quiet now, as I couldn't forget what Geraldine had said to me. I heard Samuel's voice outside the door. I stood with my cup of tea, and peeked out the window. When I did, my stomach twisted into knots. It was Aaron.

• • • • • • •

The first time I met Aaron, he'd come riding to my old house with Samuel. Matthew had gotten in trouble in school for licking a boy who'd taunted my Hannah. A few days after the school incident, my husband had been drinking all weekend, and was passed out in our bedroom, when a knock came on the door. I'd answered, and been introduced to both Aaron and Samuel. They were stern, yet kind.

When Aaron asked questions, he expected straight answers. I had no reason to hide the reality both Hannah and I faced, as long as the Stanley brothers were discreet. I had always liked Aaron. He was a good-natured man who loved his family, even if he tended to be quite sober.

Aaron had been a steady help to me over the past year, and he and I had always gotten along well. He was my friend's husband, and a good man, taking care of Ma and his younger siblings. When the snow flew, he'd take care of his own wife and farm, then traipse through the cold to come and be sure Ma had what she needed as well. But though he was a good man, he was stern. Hannah and Matthew respected him, and everyone looked to him as leader of the family.

So it came as no surprise to me that Pearl wasn't allowed to speak to me after I'd slapped her. I knew he was fiercely protective. What I didn't know was how I could ever get back into Aaron's good graces.

I would not wait for him to enter the cabin. I would go to him. I placed my cup of tea on the table, stood, and marched to the door of the cabin.

"Now, Ruth," Ma began, and I shook my head.

"No," I said. "I need to talk to Aaron."

She clucked her tongue and shook her head, and I heard Geraldine fussing in the background behind me, but I ignored them both, opened the door, and marched outside.

Samuel was leaning up against a bale of hay outside the barn, and I had one brief, heart-fluttering moment. His sleeves were rolled up, revealing his tanned, muscled forearms crossed on his chest. His jaw clenched as he chewed a piece of straw, and his hat shaded his face. He was all man, raw muscle and power and strength, and it hit me hard before I renewed my courage and plowed on.

When I came to them, Samuel's eyes met mine and narrowed. He shook his head once, one curt side-to-side shake, and he pointed a stern finger back to the house, making a scooting motion with his fingertips. I knew he didn't want me confronting Aaron now, but I had to do what I came for. Swallowing, I ignored Samuel, and walked straight up to Aaron.

He was adjusting the reins, smoothing one large hand over the rippling flank of his horse, as he walked her to the barn. His hat also kept his face in shadow, and his large form moved with grace and purpose. I felt my bravado nearly fail me.

"Ruth," Samuel warned.

I suspected I would regret ignoring him later, but it was a risk I was willing to take.

He was just about by the barn, still talking to Samuel.

"Have you noticed anything else missing?" Aaron shouted over his shoulder. He still hadn't seen me.

Samuel shook his head, pushing one foot off the hay bale and marching on over to me. "Not yet," he said to Aaron. I moved quickly away from him. He was going to make me go in the house and I would not go.

"We had some chickens stolen last week," Aaron said over his shoulder. "And it looks like eggs are being taken. Thought it was just a poacher, but now that you know someone's stolen property, could be somethin'—" He froze as he turned around and saw me.

Samuel glared at me, not trying to be discreet anymore. "Ruth, get back in the house," he ordered.

I shook my head sadly at him. I would not obey. Not this time. "I have to speak to Aaron."

Aaron drew himself up to his full height, meaning he towered over me, and he took one step closer. "Ruth," he said with a stern nod.

I drew in a shaky breath and curtsied politely. I believe it very well may have been the first curtsy I'd ever done in my life. I saw Samuel shake his head and his eyes roam heavenward.

"I need to speak to you about last week," I said.

Aaron's jaw clenched, his eyes narrowed, and his arms were tight across his chest as he eyed me. He said nothing, merely nodded.

"You know I... just wanted to explain..." But I could hardly say the words out loud. My eyes dropped to the ground.

"Say it." It was Samuel, not Aaron. I lifted my eyes and

looked at him in surprise. He looked every bit as stern as Aaron now.

I sighed. I'd disobeyed him staying out here and approaching Aaron when it was likely not a good time to do so, and now he'd make me do what I came for.

"Go on. You insisted on bringing this up? Tell him what you did last week."

Drawing in another shaky breath, I continued. "I lost my temper with Pearl." The words hung suspended in the air, and I wanted to take them back.

"And?" Aaron said. "Why don't you tell me in your own words why you lost your temper, Ruth."

I folded my hands behind my back to keep from fidgeting, and nodded. "Yes, sir." I never called any man *sir* unless it was Samuel after he'd spanked me and made love to me and I was as subdued as a church mouse, but now I pulled out anything I could think of. I inhaled. Better to get it all out at once. "She told me I wasn't thankful for all the work that Samuel's done for me, and it made me angry." I swallowed as Aaron raised his brows. "I don't always like the idea that people are helping me. I like to do things on my own. I want to prove that I can."

Aaron nodded. "She told me. She had no right to lecture you about that, Ruth, and I've spoken to her about it."

I nodded. "Well, after she said that, I lost my temper. I didn't mean to, Aaron. I've never done it before. But I slapped her right across her face."

He nodded, his eyes darkening. "Oh, I know it," he said. "I came home for supper and my wife had the traces of a handprint straight across her face. How do you think I felt about that, Ruth? To work all day and come home to my wife, heavy with child, with evidence someone'd struck her?"

"I bet you were fit to be tied," I said softly, casting my eyes down again.

"Oh, I was. The only thing that stopped me from comin' out to give you a piece of my mind was Pearl beggin' me to be merciful. So I did. This time. But damned if I'll let you near her again. You say this is your first time hittin' someone, yet I was there the day you tossed water in Geraldine's face. Seems you're given to temper more than you care to admit these days." He frowned at me.

I squirmed. It was true, and I wanted to tell him it wasn't. But I couldn't. I *was* given to temper more recently, and my actions had surprised even me.

His eyes softened a bit as he continued. "Now, I know you had one difficult situation, Ruth. I knew Leroy and I know what he was capable of. You've done good, makin' a way for yourself, and takin' care of your daughter. But you do understand that until I know you're not gonna lose your temper again, I'm keepin' my wife in her delicate position away from you."

My heart sank. I turned to Samuel. "Tell him, Samuel! Tell him how I already paid for what I did."

Samuel was frowning at me now, too. "Oh, I did," he said. "When he told me you oughtta be spanked for such a thing, I told him clearly I'd already taken care of that and you'll continue to answer for your disobedience."

Suddenly I was mortified, and I wanted to run away and hide. My cheeks flamed, but I had to speak my mind. "I'm trying hard, Aaron. I *asked* Samuel to take me over his lap. I wanted to pay for what I'd done, and I did. Won't you give me another chance?"

Aaron worked his jaw for a minute as he looked from me to Samuel. "Not today, Ruth," he said, gently but still firmly. "Not when she's about fit to bustin' with that baby. She needs to take to bed and ease her discomfort." He shook his head. "Not today." He turned his back to me, effectively dismissing me as he turned back to Samuel. They spoke in low murmurs while I stood back.

Aaron swung himself up on the back of his horse, tipped his hat to me, and took off at a trot toward town. My heart sank within me. He was not going to allow me to see Pearl. My only real friend, heavy with child, and I wouldn't be able to help her when she needed me. I wanted to cry.

Samuel beckoned for me to come to him. I dragged my feet, as I knew I'd disobeyed him. But when I reached him, he put his arm around me and hugged me.

"I know this is hard for you," he said. "And I think Aaron's bein' a bit harsh. But the best way for this to blow over is not to stir it up but let it lie. You understand?"

I nodded.

"And why do you think I wanted you not to come out here right now?"

I sighed into the fabric of his shirt, the roughness somehow soothing against my cheek. "You knew he wasn't going to want to listen to me," I said sheepishly.

He continued. "Did I tell you not to talk to him right now? Did you know I wanted you back in the house?"

I couldn't deny it. "I did."

"And yet you plowed on anyway."

"I had to! I had to tell him my side!"

Samuel frowned. "I didn't tell you not to speak your mind. It was the timing that was wrong. You should've listened to me."

My temper rose, this time because he was right and I'd been wrong. I was angry at myself for making a bad situation worse and I didn't know what to do with that anger. "Well, you don't always know everything," I muttered.

His eyes flashed at me. "Adding disrespect now, Ruth? First you disobey and now you sass me?"

I looked away, wishing I could stop myself from spinning out of control.

Samuel continued. "Aaron was fit to be tied over that saddle bein' missin', and his own things being pilfered, and in no mood to be merciful or compromise. You ought to remember that, woman. When a man has somethin' troublin' him, he's unlikely to be merciful. You understand my meanin'?"

I nodded slowly. I thought I understood. I dug the toe of my boot in the ground nervously. "You're not feeling merciful at the moment, are you?"

He shook his head, his grip tightening. "Not at all."

• • • • • • •

He marched me to the barn, holding my elbow tightly, and I had to skip to keep up with his long strides. He pulled out his milking stool, and pointed a finger for me to sit. Why was he making me sit? But after I obeyed him, I watched as he walked to the edge of the barn and over to a young birch several yards away from the barn door. I gasped. He meant to cut a switch? I watched him, my mouth gaping open, as he removed a thin switch with a knife and stripped it. He marched back to the barn, stern conviction written across his features.

"Come here, please," he said, gesturing to the half wall that separated the loft from the stalls. It stood about as high as my waist. I stood and walked to him on trembling legs. When I reached him, his hand went to my jaw and he looked me straight in the eyes.

"You were rude to me, and disobeyed me," he said. I nodded as he continued. "I was trying to protect you. I was trying to save you unnecessary hurt. How can I do that if you don't obey me?"

"You can't," I whispered.

His eyes darkened as he released my chin and pointed to the wall. "Lift your skirts and lower your drawers. Then lean across that wall."

I obeyed quickly. I needed it over with. I knew he wouldn't spank me too hard, but I also knew a switching would sting and I was eager to get to the point where we were reconciled once again. He'd tried to protect me. My thoughts and emotions were nearly strangling me. I needed to be set to rights again.

As my drawers fell to my ankles, a breath of air hit my bare skin. I was mortified, while at the very same time there was something darkly erotic about being bared to him, prepared to receive my punishment. I bent obediently over the wall as he stepped over to me, placing a hand on my lower back.

"With each stroke of this switch, I want you thinking about how much I care about you. While every one of my instructions to you may not always make sense, they are *always* made with your best interest in mind. Do you understand me, young lady?"

My eyes were squeezed shut as I braced myself for the first stinging swat. "Yes, sir."

The switch whistled through the air and struck me hard, the pain intensified in such a small area, it flared across my bottom. Again, the switch fell. I came up on the tips of my toes as a third swat landed.

"You'll do what I say," he said soberly, with another whistling lash of the switch. "You'll learn to be respectful. You'll learn to obey me." Swat after swat fell and I lost count, the switch *whooshing* through the air right before searing pain blossomed. A cry rose in my throat and tears threatened to spill. He paused, his hand resting on my tender skin.

"Have I made my point, little Ruth?" he asked.

I nodded my head, my cheeks hot with embarrassment. "Yes, sir," I whispered.

He yanked up my drawers, dropped my skirts, and pulled me to his chest, tossing the switch to the side. His eyes were grave, but filled with concern. I felt contrite now, and as I thought about Aaron not letting me see Pearl, the tears that welled in my eyes began to fall. I felt sorry I'd disobeyed Samuel and earned a punishment, sorry that I couldn't see Pearl, and heartbroken that I'd not met the expectations of the family I loved so dearly.

His eyes softened. "Come here now, honey," Samuel said, leading me to the milking stool in the corner. He sat and pulled me onto his lap, holding me tightly. "You deserved that and you know it," he said. "You get riddled with guilt sometimes, and the best cure for that is a clean slate. I'm not angry anymore. And I know this is hard for you, but I must insist you obey me. You understand why?"

I nodded. "Yes, sir," I sniffled. "You want to make sure I obey you so you can watch out for me."

"That's exactly right, honey," he said. "You need to trust me. All your life you've never had someone to trust, now have you?"

My tears started afresh. I could merely shake my head.

"Will you trust me now, then, little Ruth? Do what I say, and I'll do right by you. I give you my word."

"I'll trust you," I whispered. Still sniffling, I held onto his shirt, feeling his warm, strong arms about me, his kiss at the top of my head protective and soothing. "I promise, Samuel, I will do my best."

"And that's all I'm askin'," he whispered in return.

His hand traveled the length of my hair, smoothing everything back and tucking stray hairs into the bun at the nape of my neck. When he reached my neck, his strong hand wrapped around it, holding me even tighter than before as I felt the tears begin to diminish.

"Shhh," he said. "It's all right now."

"But it won't be," I wailed. "Aaron hates me! He won't let me near Pearl. I can't do right!"

"Course you can, honey," Samuel said. "You know it'll all work out. Just right now, he needs a little time. He's got a wife about to have a baby, and a home to ready for his family, responsibilities here, and much that must be done. It's their first baby, and the proud papa needs to make sure everything's in place. He's not happy about the theft, either. It indicates somethin' brewin'."

I nodded. He was right.

"But Ruth?"

I looked at him as he took my chin in his hand.

"You'll stay away. You'll mind Aaron's decision, or you'll answer to me. Am I clear? You go over there, and I'll whip your backside proper. You understand me?"

I nodded as a shiver went over me. Still sore from being

spanked, but yet attracted to how stern he was with me. I couldn't help it. I loved him for it.

"Samuel? Are you sure that he'll soften over time?"

"I'm sure of it, honey," he said.

I, however, was not so sure.

• • • • • • •

I went back to my home later that afternoon with a heavy heart. Ma had tried hard to talk me into staying for supper with Hannah, but I needed to be alone. I needed some time to think. So I met Hannah coming out of school, and we walked in amiable silence until we were near our house.

"I saw Pearl in town today, Ma," Hannah said.

"Oh?" I asked, my head kept down, eyes on the dirt road in front of us.

Hannah nodded. "I said hello, and she nodded, but she was a bit different. Distant-like. Why, Ma?"

I sighed. "Pearl and I got into an argument," I said simply. No need to get into the details.

Hannah nodded. "Matthew and I got into a fight today too," she said.

"Oh?"

"Yep, I busted his nose and that settled that."

"Hannah!" I was so shocked I froze. I turned to her, my mouth agape. "You didn't!"

Her eyes darkened. "Sure as shootin' did, Ma."

I blinked, not sure how to continue for a minute, before I found my voice again. "Why, Hannah? Why ever would you do such a thing?"

"He tried to kiss me!"

I bit back a bark of laughter and instead managed to cover it up with a cough. "Did he?" I murmured. "Well, then. I bet you learned him, huh?"

"Oh, I did," she said, nodding her head vehemently. "That boy won't be tryin' to kiss me anytime soon."

I chuckled ruefully, hoping her words would prove prophetic at least for another few years. "Well," I said, "you and I are bound to make sure the Stanleys think we're a fierce breed, now, aren't we?" I shook my head. "But they're our friends, Hannah. We need to be kind to our friends."

"I don't go around kissing my friends!"

She had a point. "All right, then, darlin'. You have my permission to smack him if he tries to kiss you again."

"All right."

We turned then to the sound of hooves pounding hard on the trail. We pulled to the side, as the sound often indicated a horse was moving at a breakneck speed. I started when I saw it was Matthew. He drew the reins on his horse, coming to an abrupt stop.

"Where's the fire, Matthew?" I asked.

"Oh, no fire, Miss Ruth," he said. "But it looks like Pearl's baby is comin' sooner instead'a later. I've been asked to fetch the doctor."

My eyes closed briefly. How I longed to go to her, to comfort her and to help her. But I could not.

"Go, then, boy," I ordered. I watched the horse gallop off, as Matthew tipped his hat, and I wondered if there was anything at all I could do. I finally determined that after my earlier conversation with Aaron and the punishment from Samuel, I would do as I was told.

I sighed. Childbirth was painful and dangerous. I longed to go to Pearl. Could I, even knowing I risked the wrath of both Aaron *and* Samuel?

• • • • • • •

I could not disobey Samuel. I *would* not, no, not even if my limbs longed to run. I had to obey him as it was the only way to prove to him he could trust me. He had forbidden me from contacting Pearl until Aaron gave me leave. So I would do my very best to obey.

Hannah and I made it back to our cabin, and I busied

myself with the monotonous routine of cleaning and meal preparation. I sliced our bread and served the cold chicken I'd already cooked. We ate while Hannah regaled me with tales from school, the way Matthew amused the girls by walking the fence backward with his eyes closed. I shook my head. That boy was incorrigible. He'd dipped Hannah's braids into ink and tried to write with them like the top of the quill. Hannah had managed to get away, and I wondered if the kissing incident had been before or after the attempted hair dipping. It didn't matter. That my little girl refused to be cowed by a boy *did* matter, and I was proud of her, though I still wondered if her protestations would end her in trouble.

It was only a matter of time before she'd get in trouble in school, or stop fighting Matthew's actions. I was grateful for the distraction of her chatter as my mind wandered, wondering how Pearl was. Was she in agony? Had the baby come? Had anyone been there to help her? These questions and more plagued me.

I rarely scrubbed the floor in the evenings, since the light was so poor, but now I could hardly stop myself. I got down on my hands and knees, while Hannah worked over her primer, scrubbing and scrubbing, taking out all my fears and frustrations on the floor until it gleamed in the light of the lantern.

So many questions, so few answers.

Was Pearl all right? Would Aaron let me go to her when the baby came? How could I show him I was not a threat to her?

Would Samuel intervene for me? Was his family safe from those that were predators?

But the one question I put off time and time again, finally came to the forefront.

What was happening between me and Samuel?

Night was falling, and I took my lantern to do my nighttime chores by the barn. Hannah was tidying up inside, her schoolbooks tucked away. It was still only dusk, the sky darkening, and the tree limbs and branches were stark against the night sky. Our livestock was well fed and watered. I was weary, and it was time to get ready for bed. But as I turned to go inside, I heard the pounding of hooves on hard earth. It was Matthew, riding as if his life depended on it.

CHAPTER SIX: NEW LIFE

"Matthew!" I said. "What is it?" I knew something was horribly wrong.

"It's Pearl," he said.

"Go on."

He slung himself down from the horse. "Somethin' about her waters breakin'. Ma was goin' to her, but just after she got supper ready to go, she felt faint herself. I had her lie down, and she's ill, Ruth. Not a tiny bit, but truly ill. I don't know what's the matter with Ma, but there ain't no one to help Pearl. We tried to get the doctor, but he's visitin' family or some such. "

Ma often functioned as the town midwife, having delivered dozens of little babies to our bustling town. She'd helped Geraldine deliver her baby, and now Pearl needed her. But how could she help if she were sick?

I nodded. I couldn't leave Hannah alone, though. I thought briefly of the rustling in the barn, the saddle gone missing from Samuel's stores, and my little Hannah alone in the house. I was already running to the stable.

"Matthew, you fetch Hannah and bring her back to your house. I'll ride alone to Aaron's."

I'd been strictly forbidden to go to Aaron and Pearl's,

but I didn't care if Samuel whipped me until I couldn't sit properly for a month. I would go to Pearl when she needed me, and deal with the overbearing Stanley men later.

I saddled up my horse and watched as Hannah sat astride Matthew's. I followed them, all of us at a gallop, Hannah hanging onto Matthew ahead of me. I wondered if Ma was okay, if she'd fallen ill so quickly. It was the harsh reality of our existence. Though my own family had fared well when I was younger, I'd seen many a traveler on our caravan headed west take ill and be buried in the ground before nightfall. My mother buried babies, and Geraldine had as well. My own grandmother had been taken by consumption; my pa's brother plagued with fever an' ague; my youngest cousin, just knee high to a grasshopper, bit by a rattler and cold by nightfall. Illness meant uncertainty. Childbirth did as well.

I felt the chill of fear creep along my neck, and the reins slipped in my sweaty palms. We didn't have far to travel, just through the town, which was quiet and unoccupied in the evening like this, save the lone light from the saloon. The only sound was the pounding of horse's hooves, and my own panting.

I caught a gleam out of the corner of my eye, and turned slightly to the side, but it was difficult to see anything with the jostling of the horse, my legs wrapped around her flanks. It was unusual for anyone to be out in the evening, unless they were paying a visit to the saloon. Someone, or something, was hiding in the woods. I thought of Samuel's missing saddle, and I tried to get a better look, but when my eyes flickered on the place in the forest where I'd seen something shining, the view I'd gotten disappeared. I couldn't focus on that right now. I had to get to Pearl.

Pearl and Aaron's home was a snug place nestled just behind Ma's and adjacent to Geraldine and Phillip's. It was a good enough distance away that they had privacy from the rest of their family, but close enough that travel was easy between the two homes. I could see a lamp burning at Ma's, and another at Pearl and Aaron's. Matthew and Hannah veered off, and I mentally thanked Matthew for taking care of my girl.

I continued on to Aaron and Pearl's. When I arrived, I pulled up the reins to bring my horse to a halt. I flung myself down from the saddle and affixed the reins to the post. I patted my horse's flank. "Good girl," I whispered. "You did good."

Straightening my spine, inhaling deeply, I stepped toward the entrance to their home. I'd visited many a time, but I'd never been an unwelcome guest. I knew Aaron was fastidious about the latch being fixed tight, but as they were expecting someone to come help Pearl, I hoped the door would be open. It was. I knocked to alert them of my presence, then gingerly pushed it open and stepped inside. I didn't want to startle them, but time was pressing.

All was dark but for the small circle of light from the lantern. I could hear them in their bedroom, and hastened to go to them.

When I came to the door of their room, Pearl was lying in bed, moaning, her eyes shut tight, and Aaron's arm was around her shoulders. He looked positively stricken, his face white as a sheet as he whispered in her ear.

"Aaron? Pearl?" Pearl's eyes flew open and Aaron whipped his head to me at the sound of my voice.

"Matthew came for me," I said as explanation. I turned to Pearl, knowing she might not yet know what was happening. "It seems Dr. Gentry is not home, traveling or some such. No one could find him, and Ma is in bed sick."

"What's the matter with—" she began, then closed her eyes and grasped the sheets, moaning out loud. Aaron smoothed the hair from her face, but there wasn't much he could do. The pain would only come quicker and intensify until she had a baby in her arms.

"Right, then," I said briskly. "There are things that need to be done. Let's get prepared to have this baby."

"Have you delivered a baby before?" Aaron asked, his

brow furrowed.

I frowned at him. "No, I haven't. Have you?"

His eyes narrowed. "Well, no, but I've delivered calves and foals." His eyes softened a bit as he stroked his beard. "I surmise it's much the same, no?"

I rolled my eyes. Confound the man!

"Well, of course it's much the same but it isn't the *same*. Your wife needs a woman's touch now."

Pearl's face had relaxed as the spasm of pain subsided. I continued. "Aaron, you need to fetch me some blankets, and lots of them. Bring your wife a cold cup of water, too." He looked at me for a minute, and my patience failed. "For goodness' sake, will you bury whatever anger you have toward me at the moment and take care of your wife? Go!"

He left, and I heard him fiddling with the pans in the kitchen.

I heard Pearl giggling behind me. "Oh, there aren't many women who'd boss a Stanley man around like that," she said, covering her hand with her mouth. "Certainly not me. I'm impressed."

I smiled at her, but her face contorted again as the pain renewed. I held her hand as the pain consumed her.

She gasped. "Ma... Ma said sometimes the pain comes hard and fast with little break in between when the time is right, especially if the waters break, and they did."

She closed her eyes and I grasped her hand tightly. "It hurts, Pearl. I'll not lie to you. The pain is going to become more intense, but you can handle this. You are a strong woman, married to a Stanley, for pity's sake."

A smile creased her face, the calm settling briefly between contractions of pain.

"You know I've been through childbirth only once, and I don't have much experience."

"You've more'n I do," she mumbled, her eyes shut tight.

"I do. And I can tell you that this pain is awful but you can take it. You're strong. Women like me and you, we don't run from the pain." I swallowed, suddenly my cheerful words meant to encourage her becoming my own mantra, my own encouragement when all bravado would fail me. "We don't hide from pain. We don't break. We walk into the pain, and emerge victorious."

Her eyes fluttered open and she squeezed my hand. Her eyes were misty. "We do," she whispered. "Thank you, Ruth."

"Do you need anything?" came Aaron's voice outside.

"Get him busy," Pearl said. "He's nervous, and it won't do if he's too close now."

"Fire and hot water!" I shouted. "Boil water and give me the cleanest rags you can find."

When I delivered the animals, we needed hot water nearby, rags to catch the babies and clean the mess birthing would bring, and boiling a large pot of water would keep him busy.

"Good," Pearl whispered. "Help me see, Ruth. Help me see if the baby's coming soon." Her head dropped as another spasm of pain erupted, and I nestled my hand on her swollen abdomen. I could feel the muscles contracting beneath my hand.

"And these pains are coming quickly?" I asked.

She nodded. "Nary a minute in between," she whispered. "The baby's coming, and fast. My waters broke and the pain began right away, like."

I nodded. "I need to look, Pearl," I said, not exactly sure what I was looking for, and she immediately spread her legs wide, her head tipping to the side. As quickly as I could, I lifted her skirts and to my shock, a faint wisp of hair indicating the top of her baby's head was crowning.

"Lord almighty," I breathed. "Oh, my, we don't have much time. Already, I can see the top of your baby's head. This is good. Very good!" At least I *thought* it was good and I somehow thought if I said it out loud it would make it so. Once the baby's head emerged, I wasn't quite sure what would ensue.

Pearl was groaning now, writhing on the meager bedding

around her, and I pulled her to sitting up.

"It should help if you sit up," I explained. "So you can bear down. That's what I think will help, you know. Let nature work for you. Let's try that. Do you feel like you can begin pushing?"

"I feel," she began, panting, her voice rising with each word she spoke, "that I couldn't," *pant, pant*, "hold back pushing now if I tried!"

I nodded. "Push then, Pearl. Push!" I encouraged her, squatting in front of her. I looked at my hands, which I'd scrubbed clean, but they seemed still too filthy to catch a newborn baby. I rubbed them fruitlessly on my apron, wishing I had that hot water I'd asked for.

I reached one hand to Pearl's as she held on for dear life, grasping so hard I could feel the bones of my fingers grinding together. I gritted my teeth, uniting my agony with hers, and slowly, as she heaved, the top of the baby's head grew larger, emerging, and I held my breath in wonder as I witnessed the messy, terrifying, miraculous new life emerge from the woman in front of me. I knew when I was delivering a calf, the importance of making sure no part of the animal was caught, or stuck, and fortunately Pearl's little baby came easily. First, the head emerged, and a spasm stopped while Pearl caught her breath, but her body knew what to do. What seemed liked mere seconds passed before she was pushing, letting loose a final guttural scream as I caught the baby.

"You've brought another bossy Stanley man into the world, Pearl," I tsk'd. She laughed, reaching her arms to her baby. I placed him straight on her belly.

"Aaron!" I shouted. "Bring me that water!" I had to admit it felt nice telling him what to do.

The door swung open, and I heard him come in and then freeze.

His voice was a whisper. "Is she all right?" he asked. "The baby's here already?"

"She, being your wife? Oh, she's perfect," I said. "But if

the she refers to your baby, I'm so sorry, but there is no other she here. You have yourself a strapping young boy, Papa."

He placed the heavy pot of hot water on the floor and nestled a clean pile of rags on the edge of the bed. I let him and Pearl fawn over the new baby as I finished the messy job of helping her clean up—cutting the cord and washing her, helping her affix the baby to her breast, cleaning with the hot cloths.

"Hand me the baby a moment," I said gently. Pearl handed me the baby, and Aaron handed me a small, clean blanket. I used the softest cloth I could find to clean the baby's face and eyes, then swaddled him like a caterpillar in a cocoon before handing him back to his ma.

"You have a lovely boy," I said, watching wistfully as Pearl and Aaron held their precious baby close. Aaron lifted a finger and delicately traced the hair on the baby's head.

"Perfect," he said. "Are you all right?" he asked Pearl.

She nodded. "Patrick," she said. "We decided if it was a boy, we'd call him Patrick. He looks like you," she whispered to Aaron.

I couldn't tell if he looked like either one of them, as he looked like a ruddy newborn with teeny tiny features, a button nose, and little red mouth, but he was so small and sweet, his tiny arms reaching for Pearl. But Pearl saw him through the lenses of new motherhood, and she saw her man's features.

No doubt she was still in pain, and would be for some time. I knew from my own experience the after pains of her body returning to normal would still surface, but at least the most intense spasms had lessened.

I would have to remain for some time to help Pearl. She'd never nursed a wee one before, and she would need help with things around the house. For now, she'd need someone to help her clean up and get around, as it was painful to deliver a baby. But as much as I wanted to stay and help, the sudden memory that I wasn't welcome in their home returned.

I busied myself tidying up the cabin, until Aaron emerged from the bedroom.

"She's doing fine now," he said. "They both are." He leaned up against the wall and crossed his arms on his chest. "I have to thank you, Ruth. I'm not sure what I'd have done without you."

I shrugged. "Oh. Well, it was my pleasure," I said. "You know I'd do anything for her. I'm not an expert, but it seems I knew enough to help, and I'm grateful I could."

Silence hung between us for a moment before he spoke. "Seems I've been hasty, Ruth."

I folded the rags that were left out and patted the top of the pile, then picked up the broom and began to sweep the floor before I replied. "Well, you know I'm sorry for what I did, Aaron." I wouldn't look at him, and merely continued tidying up. My hands needed to be occupied. "I know you were angry, and I don't blame you. I shouldn't have done what I did. But you also need to know I'm sorry." I placed the broom up against the wall and faced him. He was working his jaw, arms still across his chest.

"You answer to Samuel now," he said.

I blinked, looking at him, confused as to why he'd brought this up seemingly out of nowhere. "I... well, yes, I suppose I do," I said awkwardly. I shifted on my feet, not knowing exactly what he meant by "answer to."

He nodded briefly. "He'll be good to you, Ruth. Some women are strong, and fiercely independent. You know that. One of the strongest women I know is lying in bed with a new baby in her arms."

I waited patiently for him to continue, as my heart swelled with pride for my friend.

His voice softened a bit as he continued, his amber eyes piercing mine. He reminded me of Samuel in that moment—brave and stern, but kind. "And sometimes, what a strong woman needs is a man just that much stronger than she is." He uncrossed his arm and pinched his thumb and index finger together, indicating 'just a little' with his fingers. "Just *that* much stronger. And when she finds that man that can take her on, she is free to be who she needs to be. She doesn't worry about things that aren't hers to worry about anymore. She's free to let go and trust. And if he's willin' to take you on, he'll be happy he did."

My face broke into a grin. It was the best gift he could've given me. My voice was oddly husky, my eyes damp. "It seems he's willing," I whispered.

He grinned back. "I know it, darlin'."

I nodded.

"And Ruth?"

"Yes?"

"You come on back here and help Pearl with the new baby, all right?"

Relief flooded through me at the words. "Thank you, Aaron. I will."

"Now I'm gonna tend to my wife and son," he said with a great deal of pride, "and you rest here and wait for Samuel. No goin' back alone, hear? He'll come for you."

I agreed, but as he went back through the door to Pearl, I wondered at his words.

Would he? Not just now, but would he be the one for me? Was he willing to 'take me on'?

CHAPTER SEVEN: "WHO'S THE ONE IN CHARGE HERE?"

I loved being with Pearl and her new baby. Loved it. I'd so missed having a little one around, and forgot about the sweet little baby coos and sighs, the teeny fingers that wrapped my own as I sat in the rocker and rocked while Pearl slept, the way he felt light as a feather in my arms. He was a sweet little thing, quiet and gentle. My own Hannah had been fussy for a time, but I'd still known nothing sweeter than sitting by the fire, rocking a sleeping baby.

Aaron was busy in the field, tending to the spring crops, and Samuel came by occasionally. I spent every day with Pearl, helping her learn how to nurse her baby, cooking her meals, and cleaning her house. I was happy to help, and eager to make amends for what had happened, but I spent more time there than I did my own home. Hannah came with me when she wasn't in school, but my own crops needed tending, and my own house needed upkeep. After a week spent with Pearl, Samuel came by one day, just before dusk began to fall. I'd missed him, and was happy to see him. He removed his hat, shook it, and hung it on a peg by the door.

"How's the new mama and baby?" he asked.

"Oh, thriving," I said, stirring the soup on the stove. "Pearl is feeling stronger every day, and little Patrick is growing like a weed. How's Ma?" I'd gone to visit her the day before, bringing her some homemade soup, and she'd improved quite a bit.

He folded himself into a chair at the table, and when I glanced at him, my heart gave a little thump. His legs were apart, hands folded lightly, his broad lap manly and welcoming. His sleeves were rolled up revealing the tanned, muscled forearms I'd come to love. His blue eyes twinkled at me. I wanted to drop the spoon and run to him, snuggling myself up on his lap, but Aaron was right outside and Pearl just in the other room.

He shrugged. "She's better," he said. "Seems she caught some sort of stomach sickness, but is taking food and water now, back up on her feet. Geraldine's been by daily takin' care of the house and meals." He paused. "You girls are good like that, takin' care of each other."

"It's the way we do things," I said.

"Is that right, little Ruth?" His voice had dropped, and I could hear it, the *come hither* laced deep in his low voice.

I stirred the pot, the spoon swirling rapidly, faster than it needed to, from sheer nerves. My heart tripped in my chest.

"Why, yes," I said. "We always help one another. It's the way of the world on the prairie. Kin and the like, when one is out, the other takes over."

"Takes over, is it?" he murmured.

I placed the spoon down and turned around to look at him. I gave a little yelp when I realized he was standing right behind me, having prowled up to me like a cougar to its prey.

"Samuel Stanley!" I hissed, swatting my hand at him. I was careful to keep my voice down lest I disturb the new mama and her baby. "You shouldn't scare a woman like that!"

"Oh?" he asked, prowling closer.

"Oh!" I responded. "It's not right—"

One of his hands wrapped around the back of my neck, a move that had become familiar and welcome, drawing me close to him as his mouth met mine. His tongue plundered my mouth, and my legs trembled. Fortunately, his strong arm behind me brought me closer to him, holding me tight and steadying me. I sighed into his mouth as we kissed, though part of me feared being caught. What if Pearl came out of the room, or Aaron in from the field? But I pushed away my fears and discomfort. It felt so nice being held like this. It had been far too long.

When we finally pulled away, I circled my arms around his neck, embracing him, standing up on my tiptoes. His arms wrapped around my waist, returning the hug. I loved the feel of his arms about me. He dropped his head, and his voice came to my ear.

"I've missed you," he said in a husky whisper.

"Why, Samuel, I've been here all along and you know it."

He chuckled into my ear. "I do. But you've spent enough time here now. Geraldine comes next week to help. Aaron can do plenty around here, and you have your own home that needs tendin' to." Oh, he was right. I *did*. Still, Pearl needed me.

"Samuel, I'm still needed here."

His hand gripped the back of my neck and he tilted my face to look up at him. I felt the tingle all the way down my spine. I swallowed, trying to summon as much bravado as I could. His eyes narrowed slightly. "I know you are, and I'm also aware that you just got back into Aaron's good graces again. But heed me, woman. Your home needs tendin' to. Your Hannah's been fine, spendin' time with Matthew and helpin' in her own way with Ma, and I know she's been here often. But you're needed back at your home now." His mouth dropped so that he spoke in my ear. "*I* need you. And I need you alone."

Oh, *my*. My knees wobbled as I felt his words trickle

down me like wax dripping hot from the candle's flame.

He nodded and spoke again in my ear. "So much."

"I'll be back soon," I whispered. "I told Pearl I would—"

"You'll be back *tonight*."

I felt a twinge of irritation at his utterly predictable highhandedness. "And what if I say no?" I responded, every bit as much irritated as I was eager to hear his response, ready for my body to zing with excitement. I'd already told Pearl I'd make my biscuits for her, and my biscuits were everyone's favorite. At the same time, I liked prodding him, pushing him to take me on, pushing him to make me mind him.

Samuel's hand tightened on my neck. "If you say no?" he asked, his voice dangerously low. "You don't say no to me, and you know that, woman. What happens if you defy me, little Ruth?"

I squirmed, my voice hitching as my breath caught. I whispered my response. "I get in trouble."

One of his hands traveled down my back as his other still grasped my neck, and when he reached my bottom, he squeezed so hard I squealed.

"What kind of *trouble* do you get into, honey?" he asked. "Tell me."

"Big trouble." I wanted to push. I wanted to prod. His hand squeezed so that now it was painful, punishing.

"Tell me *exactly* what happens before I'm forced to give you a reminder right here in their cabin," he ordered. That scared me. No way did I want to be taken across his knee with Pearl right in the other room.

I gasped. "You spank me."

He nodded slowly. "I gave you an instruction, little Ruth," he said low. "Now you have one minute to obey me, before I hold you over my knee, lift those skirts of yours, and redden your sweet little bottom for all to see." He sobered. "I mean every word. Am I clear?"

"Yessir," I whispered. He released me and I staggered a

bit, heady from the rush of his words and instructions. He took me by the elbow and led me to where Pearl was with the baby in her bedroom.

"Knock on the door and tell her you need to go home."

I sighed and began to waver. I didn't make a move to obey at first. He took me by the elbow, spun me around, and delivered a crisp swat to my skirt-clad backside. I squealed, muffling the sound with my hand over my mouth.

I glared at him. He glared back, pointing a bossy finger at the door.

"*Now.*"

I knocked on Pearl's door, tossing a final glare over my shoulder, and heard Pearl's, "Come in!" from the other side. I opened the door and entered. Her baby was sleeping peacefully, swaddling in a little blanket, up against her chest.

"Are you going home now, Ruth?" she asked with a smile. Even though she looked tired, she beamed at the sweet baby nestled up against her bosom.

"I need to," I said. "I have some things to do back at the house. I know you may still need some help here—"

I heard Samuel clear his throat behind me.

"But *someone* says it's time to go back home," I said.

She smiled. "Oh, I know all about that," she said. "Don't worry about us here. You've done more than you needed to already, and Aaron and I will forever be grateful." I walked to her, running a light finger over her baby's sweet head, tucking in a wisp of hair, as she continued. "I'm so happy that you were the one with me in all of this, and that Aaron's letting you be with me again. That was so hard, Ruth. I missed you terribly."

Tears pricked my eyes as I bent and kissed first her cheek, then the baby's. "And I missed you. I'll see you tomorrow?" I thought better of it the second I said it. "I mean, maybe." I raised my voice. "Unless *somebody* gets it into his head not to let me come."

She nodded and grinned. "Any time, honey. Be good."

I smiled. "You, too." I bent and kissed her cheek one

last time, then took my leave.

Samuel was waiting outside her bedroom, arms crossed again, and one foot leaning against the wall. He crooked a finger at me. I wondered if he'd heard my references to his bossiness. Ducking my head, part of me hoped that he hadn't heard my comments about him, but a deeper, more buried part of me, hoped he had.

• • • • • • •

When we left the house, we could see Aaron returning from the field. I'd left enough food for supper that he could easily warm for them. He approached us, wiping a hand across his sweaty brow, as we were heading toward summer now, and the weather was heating up.

"Headin' home, Ruth?" he asked.

I nodded. "Samuel says it's time for me to go," I said, trying to pin a bit of the blame on him. I still felt bad that I was leaving them when they still needed me and maybe part of me wanted to needle Samuel just a tad bit more.

Aaron nodded. "Of course," he said. "You've already gone above and beyond duty, Ruth. Thank you." He shifted his gaze to Samuel. "How's Ma?"

Samuel shrugged. "Much better. Says she's too old to be sick and to let her out of bed, but we asked her to stay put just one more day."

I could well imagine how the 'ask' went, even if it was their ma they were bossing around.

Aaron nodded, his eyes growing concerned. "You think it's just a quick illness?" he asked honestly.

Samuel nodded. "I'm sure of it. She'll be fine real soon."

Aaron nodded. "All right, I best be gettin' to my wife and son," he said. His pride made me smile, and I could almost see his chest expand.

"Oh, I'm sure they'd be happy to see you, too," I said.

He tipped his hat one more time, opened the door to the cabin, and then Samuel and I were left alone. As soon as the door shut behind him, I felt Samuel grasp my elbow, hauling me behind the cabin.

"Gettin' a little big for your britches there, little girl," he began.

"I'm not wearing britches, Samuel," I corrected, my voice rising as he tugged me harder. "And we've already gone over the fact that I'm not a little girl."

"Think I'm foolin' around, young lady?" he asked, as my skirts flew up and I found myself staring at a clump of grass, my hands flailing in front of me. "I'll give you britches," he muttered.

"Samuel!" I gasped. "*Stop*! Someone will see you!"

"And well they should," he said. "Let them see what happens to a woman who acts like a petulant little girl. It's high time you felt my palm against your backside."

He landed one hard wallop.

"*Ow!*"

"Are you going to come with me now, where I can keep you safe, or do I need to warm your bottom proper?"

I wanted him to take me home and do more than spank me.

"I'll be good!" I promised.

He landed one final swat. My skirts dropped down, and he spun me around to look at him. His eyes were stern yet somehow still twinkling. His hand traveled to my chin and yanked firmly but not harshly. "Now, are you going to obey me, honey?"

I felt moisture pool between my legs, my arousal flaming within me. If he'd laid me down on the grass and taken me there, I'd not complain. I was melting, my insides warmed, ready for him to take me so badly I was nearly desperate.

"I'll obey you," I moaned, rubbing my backside and frowning for good measure.

He grinned darkly. "Very good. Let's get you home."

● ● ● ● ● ● ●

I couldn't prepare supper fast enough. I whipped through Hannah's primer and schoolwork with her while she readied herself for bed. Dinner was a simple affair of bread and eggs, and Samuel tucked in as if taking me in hand had somehow stoked his appetite. He pushed himself away from the table when he was done.

"Appetite satisfied?" I asked.

He took a long pull of water from his cup. "One is," he said low. I clenched my thighs together, just as Hannah came in from her bedroom. She pulled out a chair and sat down, getting out her books. I felt the tension between me and Samuel as if it were a palpable presence, each sway of my hips met by his hungry eyes, every flex of his muscles as if meant only for me.

"Look at you, growing like a weed," I said to Hannah as I scraped the dishes clean and cleared the table, gesturing to the floor. "There's hardly an inch left for you to swing those feet! You'll be hitting the floor by the end of the summer and we'll have to take those skirts down!" I felt a sudden pang as I thought about preparing her for school in a few months. She'd need a new dress, and new shoes, and a few small items to bring with her to school. I sighed. My crops needed tending to. Our chicks were growing rapidly, though, and soon would be laying eggs. How much money could one earn selling eggs in town, when plenty of others had their own ready supply? I worried my lip. That would be another worry for another day.

"All right, Hannah," I said. "Your evening chores are done?"

"Yes'm," she said, laying down her pencil. She yawned big and turned to Samuel. "Today, Matthew and I found a tree frog down by the creek, and named him Harvey. Then Matthew found a garden snake and had him chase the frog. The frog won this time," she said nonchalantly.

I looked at her sideways as I washed up the dishes. "Down by the creek?" I asked. "When did you go down there?"

"After school," she said with a shrug. She stood and grabbed the broom, sweeping the floor of our little cabin.

Samuel was leaning back in his chair, working his jaw, one foot propped up on his knee. "I'm not so sure I want you two goin' down to the creek unsupervised," he said. "There's been some theft in town lately, and a few new arrivals I don't trust. Aaron found evidence someone was sleepin' in his barn, and wasn't too keen on that. A few others ain't seen much but a little here and there, but with the new stagecoaches takin' off here, we've new people arrivin' daily."

Hannah frowned as she swept the floor.

"I didn't know all that," I said, turning to Hannah. "I agree. No more going to the creek without an adult. After school, it's best if you and Matthew come straight back here or go to his home. You hear?"

Hannah's eyes flashed. "I can take care of myself," she said.

"I know you can," I said, surprised at her response. She was normally easygoing and obedient. What had gotten into her? I looked over at Samuel, but he'd righted himself and his arms were crossed on his chest. He was looking at Hannah, not me.

"Your ma said not to go down to the creek without an adult. There's only one proper response, Hannah. Talkin' back ain't it. Mind your ma."

Hannah continued to frown at him, as she gazed from me to him, and a look flitted across her face.

"Hannah," I chided.

She sighed, looking at Samuel. "Yes, sir," she said, then to me, "All right, Ma."

I nodded slowly, wiping the dishes dry. "It's not that you can't handle yourself, Hannah. It's that we want to keep you safe."

She nodded, and after a moment, changed the subject. "The birds are getting so big now, Ma," she said. She'd finished sweeping and put the broom away. I'd completely forgotten about our cheeping little birds while I'd been at Pearl's.

"Time to let them go?" I asked.

"If they're ready," she said. "They may not be strong enough yet, but I think they are."

We chattered on, and Samuel amiably joined us, until it was time for Hannah to go to bed. She yawned as I brushed and braided her hair, and her eyes looked sleepy. I gave her a goodnight kiss, and she went off to her bedroom. The door shut behind her. Silence fell on the cabin for a moment.

"Come here, Ruth."

Samuel's quiet, deep voice sounded loud against the silence. I looked to him. The past few weeks, my view of him had changed. I'd always taken him for a gentle sort, and he still was, at least in part. But now I looked at his wide, strong hands and thought of them holding me down, roaming my body, or spanking me. I looked at his muscled arms, broad lap, and wide chest, and I wanted to be engulfed by him, held, ravished. When he ordered me like this, softly but firmly, my heart fluttered in my chest.

Come here.

I walked slowly to him as he watched, his stern gaze never wavering, and when I stood close enough to him so that he could touch me, he pulled me onto his lap. I sat there as he embraced me, tucking my head against his chest.

"She's never been contrary like that," I said to him.

He nodded. He dipped his head, his mouth traveling to my ear. "Been a tryin' few weeks," he said. "I know I ain't her pa, but I have no intention of goin' away, Ruth. You know that. I'm here to stay, honey, and it's well and good for children to have the guidance they need."

I nodded. I felt he was right. I couldn't have picked a better man to care for me and Hannah than Samuel, and I knew it.

"We've been alone for a while now," I said in explanation. "And it's hard for me to let some things go."

He nodded. "I know it," he said in my ear. "I think I can help you let some things go." He nipped lightly at my ear, his tongue flicking out. It was surprisingly erotic, my desire for him mounting as one hand slowly caressed my breast.

"Not here, Samuel," I whispered. "We're not alone."

"Relax," he whispered back. "I can already hear her snorin'."

I froze. He was right, Hannah's soft snores sounded in the still of night.

I was still not comfortable with it. "Please, Samuel," I said. "Take me to bed."

He gave a curt nod and lifted me straight up. "You'll never have to ask me that twice, little Ruth." He crossed the room in long strides, nudging the door open with his toe. He pushed it shut behind him with his heel, turned, and stalked to the bed. He laid me down gently without a word, his fingers unfastening the buttons that ran down the back of my dress. The fabric slipped off my shoulder.

I knew why I'd asked him in here. I knew what I wanted to do, what we *both* wanted to do, and I was helpless to stop myself.

When I was bared to him, he explored my naked body with his hands, eyes, and mouth. "What perfect breasts," he murmured, giving an appreciative flick of his tongue along one hardened nipple. My hips rose as my arousal flamed. His second hand went to my other breast and kneaded gently as his tongue continued to flick in and out. His mouth opened and he sucked a nipple in. I gasped from the sheer pain and pleasure all at once. His large hand paused at my breast, then traveled down, tracing over the curve of my hip and thigh, before moving slowly to my feminine parts. He dipped one finger into my sex. I inhaled sharply as he pumped his fingers in me. I was slick and ready. I closed my eyes, enjoying the sweet pleasure of his mouth and hands on me. With every thrust of his fingers, my arousal rose, and with every lick of his mouth, I came closer and closer to losing all control. He removed his fingers from me and knelt on the bed. I groaned, my need for him intense now. He took both of my hands and pressed them flat against my mattress.

"Keep those hands there," he ordered. I felt a stab of pleasure at the command.

I watched as he undressed himself rapidly, his shirt coming undone and falling to the floor. Next, he unfastened his belt. I swallowed, momentarily wondering what it would be like to be strapped by his belt. It was a part of him, worn at his hips and about his waist, and it seemed it would be intimate to feel what belonged to him mark me as his. I inhaled, trying to muster up the courage.

"Samuel?"

He paused, nodding to me.

"Would you ever spank me with your belt?" I asked.

The thought of a whipping with his belt was both terrifying and arousing. He paused, reaching a hand to my head, his fingers moving down until he reached the nape of my neck. He squeezed gently, but hard enough that I felt the claim in his touch. "I'll do whatever it takes to make sure you obey me." He bent down and kissed me on my cheek, a whiskery, sweet kiss. I squirmed in appreciation of the gentle gesture.

His voice was husky as he whispered in my ear. "I think sometimes you need to feel my pain to bear yours," he said. "Like you give it to me. I want you to give it to me, honey. I can take it." Unexpected tears pricked my eyes. How did he know that? I closed my eyes and nodded.

"Can you?" I whispered. Did he *know* the pain I carried?

"Yes."

I swallowed. "I'll do my best," I said.

"That's all you can do, honey," he whispered. "Tonight, give it to me. Let it go. Focus on bein' here with me now. I'm the one in control now, Ruth. Not you." To emphasize his words, he took my wrists in his large hands and pinned them up above my head.

I squirmed a bit, not because I wanted to get away, but

because when I moved, his grip tightened. I needed that grip to be strong. I needed him to be wholly in control.

His mouth traveled to my ear again. "You're not in trouble, honey," he said. "But tonight, you'll feel my belt."

My heart thudded in my chest. He released my hands, stood, and grasped the belt. I heard the clink of the buckle as he doubled it over before he crooked a finger to me.

"C'mere," he ordered, pointing to the edge of the bed. I scrambled off the bed and came to him. He flicked his finger, indicating for me to lie over the bed. I did, wondering why I'd asked for this. Was I crazy? The man was about to give me a whipping, and I hadn't avoided it but asked him to.

"Let's make sure you got my point back at the cabin," he said. I heard him drawing himself to his full height behind me, and imagined what he looked like, bare chest above the roughness of his trousers. I felt the helplessness begin to descend, and it was welcome. The whizz came through the air a split second before the sting radiated against my naked skin with a resounding *whap*.

I gasped. He paused, and I knew he was watching me for my reaction. I closed my eyes and stayed in position. I felt him move behind me and heard the whistle through the air as another lash fell. I went up on my tiptoes and grasped the quilt with my hands. It hurt, worse than his hand, but the pain wasn't unbearable. I yelped and squirmed but he held fast, pressing me into the bed, before he dropped his belt onto the bed.

"Get up on your knees," he said. I scrambled up, my bottom stinging, but excitement hammering in my chest.

"Stay right there," he growled, coming up behind me. His hands grasped my hips. I felt his mouth along my naked skin, laying gentle, fluttering kisses along my lower back and down to where he'd just strapped. I imagined he was kissing the stripes he'd just given me. "So beautiful," he murmured. "Every inch of you, for me." Another warm, sensual kiss along the curve of my spine. "So brave." A kiss on my heated skin. I felt his hand between my legs, two fingers plunging into me, almost harshly, before a finger trailed to my sensitive bud and swirled. My hips bucked, and I moaned. The short whipping he'd given me intensified my arousal. I was nearly whimpering with need now as I ground my hips against his hand. He pumped his fingers in me. I could feel myself, warm and moist against his fingers that ravished me. I was going to lose all control, but he stopped.

"N*oooo*," I moaned, arching my back toward him. I gasped as his hand connected with my backside in a sharp, corrective swat.

"Who's the one in charge here, young lady?" he asked sternly.

"You are," I said. "But I need—"

Another sharp swat.

"I said who's the one in charge here?"

"You," I moaned." You are."

He gently massaged my bottom. "Good answer."

Every touch of his hand along my skin made me quiver with desire, even when he merely smoothed his warm, rough palm along the edge of my stinging backside. Without warning, he pumped his fingers in me again. I was on the edge. I was going to lose control. I couldn't wait any longer.

"You'll wait until I say," he growled, almost harshly. "If you don't wait until I give you leave, you'll wish you had."

The threat amped me up even further, the knowledge of his belt folded over just on the edge of the bed making me grasp the quilt in my fists, holding onto every bit of self-control I had. I felt him move behind me, and heard him fumbling with his trousers, the soft rustle of fabric. I could've wept with relief. I needed him to take me.

Warm, rough hands grasped my hips. I felt his hands between my legs preparing me before he slid into me. I groaned out loud. I felt so full, so desperate for him I ground against his flank. His grip tightened. The warmth of my bottom against his skin, the residual sting of the licks he'd given me, and my body slick and ready for him, made me moan in agony. I couldn't bear it. It was delicious but torturous. Slowly, ever so slowly, he drove in and out, the measured strokes of his thrusts making me groan with need.

"Samuel," I moaned. "*Plleeease.*" He moved out and in so slowly, I couldn't breathe. My chest felt as if it were being constricted. I needed the release. The torture of his slow movements was making me lose all control and sanity. Nearly out of my mind with need, I reached a hand to his leg and squeezed. His response was a sharp crack to my bottom, which made me squeal.

"*Nooow!*" I begged him, so desperate it was a command. My hands grasped the quilt on my bed.

He withdrew himself. I moaned.

His whole body covered me, his back against mine, larger, stronger, and warm, pressing me onto the bed, my breasts flat against the roughness of the quilt, my cheek tilted to the side, my eyes closed as his mouth came to my ear.

"Who's in charge, young lady?" he whispered.

"You are," I whispered. I felt my taut body begin to loosen a bit.

"Who tells you what to do, little Ruth?" he whispered, his voice deepening.

I swallowed. It was becoming easier now, here in the dark, pinned beneath him, his warm hands holding me. "You, sir. You do." An unexpected tear escaped from my tightly closed eyelids.

I felt a kiss on my cheek, a reward for my submission.

"Who takes care of you, honey?"

"You, sir," I nearly sobbed, for he was right. He was the one who would hold my burdens. He was the one who would give me pain so that I could bear my own. And with the last shuddering breath, I let go of all control.

"Good girl," he murmured, at the very same time propping me back up on my knees. I felt every movement—his hands positioning me, every intake of his breath and mine. He plunged into me, almost harshly, but it was welcome.

"Now," he said.

It was all I needed. Ecstasy shot through me, so intense I cried out, still sniffling, the tears and bliss mingling as I soared, my mind eased from all but Samuel, his own release mingling with mine until we lay, spent, panting, and quiet in the darkness.

The tears flowed freely now. He rolled over, taking me with him, pulling me up on his bare chest.

"That's my girl," he soothed, kissing my tearstained cheeks and running a rough hand through my tousled hair. "My beautiful, strong girl."

It felt nice with my cheek against his bare chest, the small curlicues of his hair tickling my skin. I was suddenly exhausted, surrendered to him in the darkness. My eyes felt heavy.

Against my better judgment, to my shock and later regret, not as his wife, but as his lover, I fell asleep in his arms.

· · · · · · ·

I was deep in a dark, wooded area. Dried leaves crunched under my feet, and I was running, both from someone and toward someone, holding my skirts, trying to run faster, but I couldn't. The fog seemed to come to life, and I knew why I was fleeing.

Hannah.

I had to get to Hannah, and I knew she was ahead of me. I also knew that my pursuer was going to hurt me, or worse—hurt my daughter. I heard a filthy stream of words come from behind me, and I knew without looking that it was my late husband in hot pursuit. He was going to get her. I had to find her. I had to protect her. My foot snagged a tree root, and I went sprawling, my hands flying out in front of me. I screamed, but no sound came. I couldn't get to her. She would slip through my fingers and he would find her. I had to get to her.

He was upon me now, and I could feel him, though I couldn't see his rabid eyes and leering mouth mocking me. I could feel him. I could hear him, and with my next breath, his hands were on me, hoisting me to my feet viciously. I screamed out loud. And that was when I woke.

As strong hands wrapped around me in my half-asleep state, I flailed, defending myself, until Samuel's low voice came to me in the darkness.

"It's me. It's Samuel. Ruth, s*top.*"

I froze as I suddenly remembered everything. I realized I was thrashing about with a blanket wrapped around my still-naked body, and Samuel was lying next to me, holding me tightly up against him.

I exhaled, shaking my head and closing my eyes. "It was just a bad dream," I said. "An awful dream. But it was just a dream."

"Shhh," he whispered. I allowed him to hold me for a moment before I opened my eyes. As I peered over his shoulder, I saw daybreak peeking under the curtains. I bolted upright.

"Samuel!" I hissed. "Oh, you have to go! Go!" I said, pushing myself away from him in a panic.

Eyes still sleepy, he frowned. "Well, good mornin' to you, too, sunshine."

"Land's sake, if Hannah wakes up and finds you here—if Ma sees you didn't come home last night—"

He rubbed a hand across his brow, swinging his legs over the side of the bed. "Honey, no doubt Ma knows I didn't come home last night," he said in a husky, still sleepy voice.

I moaned. "She'll know that—"

"Ma keeps her own counsel," he said, pulling on his trousers and shirt. "As for Hannah, that's a fair point and I'll hightail it outta here. You watch, and we'll make sure she ain't gonna see me, all right?"

I sighed, closing my eyes. I didn't like skittering around like this. I threw on my chemise, rapidly dressing. My breathing was still ragged, my palms still sweaty as I rushed him toward the door.

"Quicker, Samuel," I hissed as he tugged on a boot. He raised an eyebrow at me, and I dropped my gaze. "All right, all right," I murmured. He smirked.

Standing, he stalked over to me and drew me close, wrapping a hand around the back of my neck, the familiar touch I'd come to expect and even crave. "I like wakin' next to you," he said low. "I could get used to that, little Ruth. I mean to make that my every day. Now you be a good girl and scoot on out to see if the coast is clear, and I'll head on home, honey."

My belly melted, my head growing light with both excitement and fear.

His every day? Waking up next to me meant he wanted to make me his.

I couldn't dwell on such things.

I raced to the door and saw Hannah's was still shut fast.

"Go, go," I hissed. "*Now.*" I gestured for him to go, but he didn't. He stalked up to me, bent down, and gave me a hard, heated kiss, his hand on the small of my back drawing me close to him. When he was done, he pulled away, spun me around, and landed a hard swat to my backside.

I glared. "What was that for?"

"For bossin' me around, woman," he said, no trace of a smile on his face. "Do it again, and I'll warm your pretty little bottom."

I exhaled and closed my eyes. I couldn't control him. He would do what he damn well wanted to, which I both loved and hated with equal vehemence. I nodded. That was when he smiled, because he knew he won. I *hmmphed.*

Taking my fingers to his lips, he kissed them before he dropped my hand, walked quickly to the door, and left. He was gone. I lifted my kissed fingers to my cheek, the conflicting emotions surrounding the entire brief morning overwhelming me. Losing Hannah in my dream. My fears leaving me as I woke up next to Samuel, followed by fear again that we would be seen. The mortifying knowledge that Ma would know he spent the night.

Suddenly nauseous, I sat down hard at the table.

I had to do something, but I had no idea what.

CHAPTER EIGHT: A PREDICAMENT

I managed to avoid visiting at Samuel's house for nearly a week, but thankfully still visited with Pearl. When Leroy was still alive, I was so isolated from everyone in our little town that I often felt alone. My self-isolation was little better. I just couldn't bring myself to look at Ma, knowing that she knew Samuel had been with me. Other folks in town might shun us, or call us out as sinners. The Stanleys kept their own counsel and would do no such thing, but they were still upstanding citizens, and every one of them were of strong moral conviction. I hated the idea of causing any of them scandal. But I also hated being separated from Samuel.

I went out by the creek, picking blueberries one morning when Hannah was at Pearl's. I wanted to bake a pie for Pearl and Aaron. I turned quickly when I heard a rustling behind me. It was not the wild animal I'd feared, but rather Ma, holding a sturdy basket with easily quadruple the amount of berries I'd picked. She blinked with surprise when I came into view.

"Why, hello, Ruth!" she said amiably. "I was just thinking about you. Whatever are you doing out here alone?"

"Same as you," I said with a laugh. "Picking berries."

"Well, I'm not alone though," Ma said with a twinkle in her eye. Samuel stepped from behind a bush then, and I started.

He bowed his head and tipped his hat to me. "Ruth," he said.

I nodded back. "Samuel."

Suddenly I felt awkward and uncomfortable, as silence fell between all of us. Samuel, however, did not appear awkward at all as he bent and kissed my cheek, then lifted the heavy basket from my hand.

"I can carry my own basket," I protested. He merely pursed his lips and raised a brow. Suddenly, I felt a pang of nausea hit my stomach, and I staggered a bit.

"You all right?" Samuel asked.

"I'm fine," I said. "I just felt a little queasy."

"Have you eaten anything today?" he asked. "Had enough water?"

I put a hand to my brow and closed my eyes, trying to remember as the nausea hit again, stronger this time, causing me to lose my footing. "I had a slice of bread this morning, and... mmm... no. No water." I opened my eyes as I tried to steady myself.

His jaw clenched and he shook his head. "We were just takin' a break, ain't we, Ma?"

She nodded, and I followed them, holding onto Samuel's arm as he led us to a shady tree. The days had grown warm as of late, and the heat made me feel even worse. I'd been wearing my bonnet to shade my face, and now it fell off, hanging about my neck by the strings, no longer protecting me from the heat of the sun. Samuel gripped my elbow and sat me down by a log, where a lunch pail was waiting in the shade.

"You'll join us for some dinner, Ruth?" Ma asked. Since Hannah would eat with Pearl, I had no need to return home to eat.

I nodded. "Thank you," I said, as another wave of

nausea rolled over my stomach. My skin felt clammy, but I tried my best to pretend I was fine. I took a slice of cheese Ma handed me, but the tangy, creamy taste had my stomach rolling. I shook my head. "I can't," I said. "I don't feel good."

"Likely you don't feel good because you haven't eaten," Samuel admonished, but Ma shook her head.

"Maybe. But it could just be that the heat is getting to be too much. It's not easy being out in the sun with these layers of clothing on, with the bonnets keeping the heat on our masses of hair."

Her words ran together as the world spun around me. I closed my eyes.

"I've got to get her back," Samuel said, standing up. "We've our wagon, Ruth. Come with me."

It felt nice not to have to think, to just know that if I followed him, he'd take care of me. I opened my eyes as my stomach heaved, the ground feeling unsteady under my feet. He bent and put an arm about my back, practically carrying me to the wagon. I felt a bit better as I sat, and I nibbled on a dry biscuit Ma had shoved into my hand.

I lifted my chin, but a wave of nausea hit my stomach again. I moaned.

Samuel's eyes grow concerned, and he frowned as he lifted the reins. "You all right, honey?" he asked with concern.

I shrugged. "I likely will be," I said. "I just got dizzy and my stomach was queasy. I'll get some water and food and will likely be just fine." We drove along the dirt road, the wagon jostling in a way that made my stomach roll harder. I did my best to clamp my mouth shut and close my eyes as he drove, trying to maintain my composure so I wasn't sick on the road.

Samuel's hand flexed on my shoulder. "When we get you home, you need to lie down," he instructed. I did not put up my usual protest. I wanted nothing more than to lie down on a cool blanket in a place that didn't bump and jostle my insides.

Finally, I heard him pull up the reins and stop the wagon, before I heard his feet hit the ground and walk to my side. Though my eyes were closed, the sounds were familiar enough that it didn't surprise me at all when I felt his hand on my elbow.

"Come here, honey," he said gently. "You'll have to stand, then lean on me."

I slowly opened my eyes, surprised at how bright the sun looked, and how the brightness made my stomach twist. I took his hand obediently, allowing him to help me down. I offered no protest as he quickly bent and scooped me up. I loved being held by him, and at the moment, nothing felt sweeter than his arms around my body. My head fell limply to his shoulder and my arms loosely encircled his neck.

"Poor girl," he murmured. "Let's get you to bed, now."

I heard the sound of the cabin door swinging open, and Samuel's firm footsteps upon the floor as he walked me to my room. He laid me gently in bed. My head fell to the pillow. I felt his fingers at my neck, unfastening my bonnet, slowly undoing the tie, then gently lifting my head to remove it. When he'd removed that, next he moved on to my feet, and I felt him slowly undoing my boots, removing them, each one clunking to the floor.

"Sit up, honey," he whispered. I tried to obey but it felt impossible. Strong arms lifted me, the buttons of my dress coming undone one at a time, then he shimmied it up and over my head.

"Good thing you have some experience helping me undress," I whispered.

His response was a low chuckle. "Good thing Ma's still out by the wagon," he said. "You'd likely regret saying that otherwise, when you come to your senses later."

My stockings were stripped, and it felt delicious wearing nothing but my thin cotton chemise on the cool of the bed. I didn't know what he was talking about, something about regret, and though it took a great effort to speak again, I had to tell him. "There's nothing I regret about me and you, Samuel," I said. My words seemed strangely heavy and slurred. "Nothing I regret."

"Hush, honey. You rest now," he said.

"Nothing I regret," I murmured again.

His mouth came to my ear and he whispered, "Good girl. That's my good girl. Now you be quiet and get some rest. Will you be a good girl and get some rest now?" I felt his hand come to my head, smoothing my hair back. I sighed. It felt so nice.

"Yes, sir," I murmured, and it took every last bit of energy I had. Darkness and heaviness descended. Reality blended with the dark, and I fell asleep.

• • • • • • •

When I woke the next morning with the light of day, at first I felt better. My head no longer hurt, and I felt stronger, no more dizziness. I stretched my arms up over my head and sat up quickly, but the minute I sat up, the wave of nausea hit me again. I looked about for Samuel, but he wasn't there of course. I fell back against the bed, lying against the bedclothes, willing the nausea to go away. I had chores to do. Someone needed to set the bread to rising, mop the floor, and bake. Someone needed to make sure Hannah was all set for school, her hair braided neatly, and her little lunch pail packed and ready. I groaned to myself. I hated that I was still sick.

Why was I sick?

It hit me all at once, and when realization hit, I felt a chill creep over me. The hair on my arms stood up on end. I felt my heart hammering in my chest, and I squeezed my eyes shut, as if somehow ignoring the reality made it all go away. I placed one hand flat against my stomach.

Maybe I wasn't sick. Maybe there was another reason for my nausea. I thought of the time frame, and with a sick realization knew then that it was entirely possible that my fears could be true.

Maybe my nights of passion with Samuel had led to something else.

I needed to do something. I needed to talk to him. I could lie there in bed, fighting the nausea, worrying so about not being able to clean, or garden, or cook, or I could deal with the fact that my reckless behavior may have resulted in a very serious consequence.

Samuel's *baby*.

The knowledge both thrilled and terrified me. What would his family think? I covered my face with my hands. What would *he* think?

I had to go to him. I needed to talk to him. He needed to know.

Ignoring the waves of sickness that overwhelmed me, I moved to go outside. I needed something cool to drink, and I needed to get out of the stuffy cabin. As I pushed through the door, the nausea overwhelmed me so badly I raced outside. Bending over a small bush outside our door, I was promptly sick. I felt better for a moment, though I was sure that if I could find a looking glass, I'd find myself looking limp and rather green. I needed to get to the water now, and today, I would have to fetch it by the well. I looked around, hoping to see Samuel, but there was no one about of course. I knew he'd have to get back to his own place. I felt a pang of regret at the distance between us.

I mean to make this my every day.

Part of me wished it already was.

It was barely daylight, and I sat next to our well, enjoying the cool morning air and the quiet, now that my nausea had abated. I filled my bucket and cupped my hands in the depths, trickling water into my mouth, and running my damp fingers along my neck. I felt momentarily better.

A baby. I thought about it. The nausea and fatigue were exactly like what I'd experienced before, when I had been expecting Hannah. What would it be like, having a child after all these years? I placed a tentative hand on my stomach and wondered.

I could no longer wait for Samuel to come on his own to me. I needed to go to him.

I hefted my bucket of water and walked quickly, placing it outside our door. I still had plenty of time before I had to go tend to Hannah. There was time to cross town and walk over to the Stanleys before the day began. The nausea still swept over me, and a few times I had to stop, though I was able to maintain my composure for a good part of the journey. I enjoyed the walk alone, the early morning sun rising as I made my way toward the Stanley house.

I knew Samuel would be none too pleased that I'd walked alone, and likely unhappy I'd even gotten out of bed. The last time I'd been at Ma's, Aaron had been telling everyone what he'd heard about the crew of men coming to town. We were a busy town, with the fur traders, and now more and more workers for the stagecoach, a new but rapidly growing business in Fort Hall. Many still traveled west, arriving at our place and deciding to travel no further. It meant our town was prospering. But it also meant new townfolk arrived daily, and unknown travelers posed a risk.

Samuel didn't even like me to fetch water from the creek alone. He'd be fit to be tied if he knew I was traveling across town alone. But I didn't care. I could defend myself, and I needed to see him. I walked as quickly as I could, and the brisk morning air seemed to quell my sickness for a bit.

When I arrived at the Stanleys, I slowed my steps. How would I fetch Samuel if he was still abed? I looked around their quiet homestead, at the stack of wood nearby, and the rows of crops. It was neat and clean, well-maintained, and it did my heart good. Hard workers lived here, and I appreciated that about them.

I tiptoed to the barn, and heard stirring within. I wasn't sure if it was the livestock or one of the Stanleys, so I peeked in as quietly as I could.

Samuel sat on a milk stool, his large frame hunched over on the small wooden stool. It was the same stool he'd sat on the day he threw me into the loft. My heart fluttered to watch him, his large hands working quickly and efficiently. The cow he was milking stirred, and he placed one large hand on her flank, murmuring something low. She stilled. I swallowed. He wouldn't be so calm when he knew I'd crossed town alone.

I stepped into the barn, hay crunching under my feet, and he looked up at me in surprise, his eyes widening.

"Ruth, what on earth?" he said. He got to his feet. "Is everything okay?"

I planned on being brave. I truly did. I lifted my chin and opened my mouth to talk. I had felt strong and courageous when walking along toward him, determined to defend myself if any danger came my way. But now, standing in front of him, with him towering over me, and his deep, steady voice traveling the short distance between us, my bravado failed. I opened my mouth to speak, but I felt my throat constrict, and no words came out. I shook my head.

He crossed over to me and put his arms around me, drawing me closer to him. "What is it, Ruth? You're still sick, honey. You should be in bed. What brings you all the way here? I'd have come to you just as soon as I was done here."

I closed my eyes, only trusting myself to whisper, my voice wavering. "Samuel…" I swallowed. I couldn't continue.

He ran one hand along the back of my head and pulled me to his chest. "Tell me, honey," he said. "Listen now, Ruth. Whatever it is, it'll be all right. Now tell me."

And I knew then that it would be. We weren't crazy young children, and he was a good man, the *best* man, the one I could trust above all others. I took a deep breath and squared my shoulders. "I don't think I'm sick," I whispered. He looked confused, shaking his head, but as I continued, he stilled. My voice still in a whisper, I said, "I think I may be with child, Samuel."

His eyes widened, and then a slow smile crept along his

face. "Do you, now?" he whispered. His hand traveled to my belly, warm and steady, the breadth of his hand nearly covering my entire stomach. "A baby? Do you know?"

I shook my head. "I don't," I whispered. "But I'm... late. And I wonder if being so tired and sick-feeling isn't related. We... well, it's certainly possible."

He grinned, lifting my chin with one of his fingers, and he kissed me. I didn't realize until his lips met mine how much I'd missed being held by him. He felt so strong and manly, and my insides melted as his hands spanned my waist with his mouth upon mine. When he pulled away, his eyes were glowing.

He didn't seem concerned at all. Wasn't he afraid of what people would say? What our future held? What would we *do*?

"When will you know?" he asked. "For sure?"

"Oh, another week or so," I said. "And I really don't know yet. I just know that I feel tired and sick, and I felt like that when I was expecting Hannah."

He nodded, and suddenly he sobered, as if he just realized I was standing in front of him in his barn. "Ruth, tell me you didn't walk across town to come here and tell me. It's bad enough you made that trip alone sick, but now thinkin' you could be with child—"

I swallowed and shifted nervously. "Well, I... had to speak to you," I began.

He made a low sound halfway between a groan and a growl. "What am I goin' to do with you, woman?" he asked. "If you hadn't just told me now that you could be with child, I'd take you straight across my knee and give you a lickin' you'd remember. You wouldn't sit for a week. How could you? Don't you know the dangers you faced?"

"I had to see you. I was prepared to face the dangers!" I protested, my heart thumping at both the threat of a spanking and the necessity of making him see my reasoning.

"Prepared to face them?" he asked incredulously. "Prepared to handle a passel of strange men who'd have their way with you? Prepared to handle the savages that roam the plains? Prepared to deal with a hungry she-bear or wildcat?" He paused. "Prepared to deal with *me?*"

I frowned at him. "Well, yes," I said.

His eyes shut briefly, and when they opened, they were dark. "Foolish woman," he said. "You'll not do this again."

I scowled at him and wanted to ask how he planned to stop me, but I knew he'd have his ways. "Samuel, I came here to tell you I'm likely carrying your child, and the first thing you do is threaten to spank me?"

He frowned. "It wasn't the first thing I did, and I'm still pleased with what you've told me. But woman, you're the most frustratin' thing known to man, and knowin' you could be carryin' my baby only makes this worse, not better."

"Fine," I said, attempting to momentarily mollify him. "But let's focus on the most pressing problem here." I paused as nausea suddenly overtook me again. The barn spun, and my stomach rolled. I felt Samuel's hands steadying me as he pulled out the stool, sat down, and drew me onto his lap. The unexpected gesture made me feel better, even as the nausea rolled over me.

"You all right, honey?"

"Just sick," I whispered. The nausea passed after a moment, and I looked up at his face. "Samuel? What are we going to do?" I asked

"About what?" he asked.

About *what?*

"About our *predicament,*" I snapped, feeling anger rising again. Confound the man!

He frowned. "Now, woman, you mind your temper. That's an easy *predicament* to solve, little Ruth."

"Is it, now?" I asked.

"Course it is. I marry you," he said, as if the answer was as simple as, say, "water the horses," or "weed the garden."

I sat up straighter. "Marry me!" I tried to shove myself off his lap but he held tight.

His eyes darkened. "Of course. Why on earth wouldn't

I?"

I had no answer.

"Woman, I've been courtin' you for weeks now. And you mean to tell me marriage hasn't crossed your mind?"

Of course it had crossed my mind, but in a way one contemplates a fantasy, not reality. I just never contemplated the fact that Samuel would really *want* me. But I had to pause at something he'd said. "You've been *courting* me? How did you do this without my knowledge?"

He snorted. "You think I kiss every pretty little thing that sashays on by me, woman?"

He'd done more than kiss me, but I'd not make a point of that. There were some things that were better not said out loud.

"You'd better not," I muttered, which made him smirk. "Well, why didn't you tell me that's what you were doing?"

"Tell you? I thought you knew," he said. "When you eat breakfast in the mornin', do you tell people you're eatin' breakfast? Course not. It's obvious. You have no pa or brother to ask, so why be all formal-like? I wanted to know if you'd have me for a husband. But if you're carryin' my child, I would hope you would know the answer to that question." His voice softened. To my surprise, he removed his hat. "There's no woman I'd rather have as my own, little Ruth. Will you marry me?"

I warmed at that. But I had to know. I had doubts. I had fears. "Are you sure you'd really want a woman like me?" I whispered.

His answer was to thread his fingers through my hair, one hand grasping the back of my neck, as he drew my mouth to his and kissed me, the fierceness of the kiss and his tight grasp on me taking my breath away. When he pulled back, I was panting. His eyes smoldered. "Does that answer your question?" he asked.

I nodded. "Even though I have a temper?"

His lips twitched. "I can handle your temper."

My voice caught at my next question. "Even though I

135

already have a daughter?"

He sobered. "I already love your daughter as if she were my own."

I closed my eyes, a lump rising in my throat. He pulled my head to his chest and held me. His voice was low when he spoke. "I love you. And I want you all to myself. Will you marry me, little Ruth?"

I nodded. And it didn't matter then if I was with child, or a spitfire, or damaged from my past. He wanted me.

I didn't know how, or when, but I knew the answer to his question. I inhaled, faced him and nodded my head. "Yes, Samuel. I'll marry you."

• • • • • • •

We heard a clattering by the barn door. I flew off Samuel's lap moments before the door opened. Matthew stood in the doorway, his hair still sticking up on end, and his eyes looking sleepy.

"Oh," he said, obviously startled to see me there. "Mornin'. You all right, Miss Ruth?"

"I'm fine, thank you, Matthew. I needed to speak to Samuel a moment, but I best be getting back to the house before Hannah needs me." I ran my hands along the length of my skirt, smoothing it out, nodding to Samuel.

Samuel handed the milk pail to Matthew. "Please take this on into the house for me," he said. "I'll be taking Miss Ruth back to her place, and giving her and Hannah a hand with their chores."

"Yes, sir," Matthew said, taking the pail and looking slowly from me to Samuel. "Miss Ruth, did you come here alone?"

Confound the Stanley line of bossy men.

"I did," I said, managing to avoid Samuel's eyes. "I had to speak to your brother, but all's good now. Thank you for the work you've done at my place, Matthew."

Matthew nodded, his eyes slightly wide. "Yes, ma'am."

"Bye now." I turned and left, lifting my skirts. I stepped quickly over the hay and into the sunshine, as it felt suddenly much too hot in the barn. Just outside the door, the sun was now rising and life was stirring upon their farm. I heard Samuel coming up behind me before I felt his hand on my elbow, steering me firmly to where we were alone, out of the view of Matthew in the barn or Ma if she came out of the cabin.

"All right, now," he said in a low voice. "The girls are comin' over today to work with Ma, and we best be gettin' you home."

"Oh, I miss them," I said. Geraldine I could take or leave, but I yearned to see Pearl. "I can just gather my things after I see Hannah off to school, and come on back. I've been so silly staying away from all of you, and I've missed you all so much."

"Well, now, that's lovely, honey. But you're not gettin' out of bed and comin' over here today."

My temper flared. "And why not?" I spat out. "I'm perfectly fine to—" I tried pulling my hand away, but he held fast. He snatched up my hand, and before I knew what was happening, he spun me around, I felt one large hand at my waist and the other landed a stinging wallop to my backside. I closed my mouth and breathed in through my nose. He hadn't spanked me hard, but merely delivered a firm reminder.

"What was that for?" I asked like a naughty child, frowning at him.

"You keep a civil tongue, young lady," he scolded. I opened my mouth to protest, and then thought better of it. Apparently my delicate condition did nothing to stay his firm hand.

"All right," I said, feeling repentant now, between the firm swat, his scolding tone, and the *young lady*. "If you insist."

We were nearing the bend in the dirt road that would

take me to my home, and still we walked in silence. My mind teemed with fears and worries. Were Samuel and I truly engaged? Where would we live? How could I marry into the family that didn't even like me? I wanted to climb back in bed and pull the covers over my head. My stomach rolled with nausea, and my hands felt clammy.

"You milk Rosy yet?" Samuel asked.

I shook my head. "I'll go now," I said.

"I'll milk her," he said. "You go see if Hannah is awake and once she is, you get yourself back in bed until I come in to check on you."

I wanted to protest. Milking Rosy was my job, and Samuel was getting awfully highhanded already. But it seemed I didn't have the strength to do it. My head felt funny and my eyes had trouble focusing. The nausea rose in my stomach, and I knew I was going to be sick again. I ran to the side of the house and heaved.

Weak from sickness, it barely registered that Samuel had followed me. I had a vague recollection of Samuel's arms about me. I remember he placed his arm about my shoulders to support me during the short walk to my room. Then everything went dark.

CHAPTER NINE: EVERYTHING
PRECIOUS TO ME

The sounds I heard in my delirium were disturbing. Voices, and screams, and sometimes low murmurs and shouts. I couldn't differentiate between what I imagined, voices of those around me, or my own voice. Images faded in and out. Hannah as a small child, her innocent face and sweet voice breaking through the shouts of my husband's drunken escapades. Ma's voice, low and soothing, and Pearl's, sweet and clear. And the one voice I longed to hear the most, Samuel's low, husky drawl. They were all voices, though, sounds, but no words.

I remember soup lifted to my lips, and water in a cold tin cup. I vaguely recall shaking my head at one point, refusing something on a spoon, shadows passing in front of me when I opened my eyes, and the low voice being the one to come to my side, whispering in my ear. Higher voices cajoling me, and it irritated me. I shook my head and shooed them away. I don't remember what I said, but I knew it was Samuel, speaking to me in the tone that brooked no argument, somehow convincing me to eat whatever was given me. I slept, and I slept, and I slept.

I dreamt of smiling, cooing babies with fetching wide

eyes, wrapped in soft blankets and nestled in my arms. Babies that had Samuel's eyes.

But when I woke up, my reality was unlike anything I'd expected. I heard voices speaking about me, and one I recognized.

"Leave her be," the voice continued. "You take Hannah out to go pick them berries you found, and be quick about it, boy. It's heatin' up here, and her ma'll want her soon."

Was it Ma? I stirred, but it seemed too much of an effort to open my eyes. I felt a cool cloth upon my forehead, and a low murmur. "Shhh, child. Rest now, love."

I sighed. It felt nice to be treated like this. Though I wished to open my eyes and move about, a part of me wished to stay here forever, under the care and concern of someone who loved me. But as much as I appreciated Ma's gentle touch, there was another I longed for.

"Samuel?" I whispered.

I was in my bed; that much I knew. I could feel the familiar quilt above me, when my eyelids fluttered open. I saw just a bit before my eyes closed against the light. I wondered if it was my bed. By the light of the window, it looked about daybreak. How long had I slept?

"Ah, she's waking up," Ma said, and I could see a low stirring in the corner. "But you stay there now. She may take a while yet."

Another cool swipe of the cloth, and I tried opening my eyes again. The light was dim, so I was able to make out that I was, indeed, in my own bed, and in the room were Geraldine and Ma, and Samuel sat in the corner. Geraldine was placing a bowl with water in it on my nightstand, and when my eyes opened, she looked at me with concern. She smiled, but then left and went about her duty.

Ma smoothed the hair off my forehead, and spoke in a soothing voice. "That's my girl," she said. "Oh, poor little one. I'll be right back. I'll fetch you what you need."

I looked about me and could only see one shadowy form in the dark room, bent over with his forearms resting on his legs, his eyes focused on me.

"Samuel?" I asked quietly. He looked haggard from lack of sleep, dark circles under his eyes, and his beard had grown in thicker than I'd ever seen. He stood, and his clothes were rumpled. He crossed the room in two long strides, and before he reached me, the door opened. Ma stood in the doorway, carrying a steaming mug in one hand and a bowl of soup in another.

"She's awake," she said to Samuel in a hushed tone, and it surprised me that she was speaking as if she didn't want to startle me.

"Of course I'm awake," I said. "Why wouldn't I be?"

She turned to face me, her eyes wide. She blinked before she spoke. "Why, Ruth," she said softly. "You've been asleep for three straight days."

I felt my stomach twist. "Have I?" I whispered. I closed my eyes and inhaled. This felt wrong. Something was wrong. I wasn't sure what it was, but it was not what it should be. When I opened my eyes, Samuel was pulling his chair over close to me. Ma handed him the bowl of soup.

They were speaking in whispers. Why were they speaking in whispers?

"Where's Hannah?" I asked.

Ma swallowed. "She's staying with me, sweetheart," she said softly, her eyes not meeting mine. "She was scared being here with you laid up, and it was easier for her to stay with us while we took care of her. Samuel stayed here with you. But Hannah's gone berry pickin' with Matthew for now. She'll be back soon."

I blinked, and it felt as if my mind somehow couldn't catch up to my ears. "Hannah isn't here," I said dumbly. "And Samuel's been with me?"

Ma smiled then as she walked to the side of the bed. She smoothed the hair from my forehead, and her voice rang with a note of pride when she spoke. "Of course he was," she murmured. "Why wouldn't he nurse his betrothed?"

My heart skipped a beat. She *knew*. I looked at Samuel,

who was merely swirling a spoon in the bowl, his jaw clenched. He looked from me to Ma, and then back to me.

"Ma, you best be getting home," he said. "Hannah and Matthew have likely finished their chores and schoolwork. It'd be time now for Geraldine to be heading home as well. I'll take over from here with Ruth."

Ma stood up straight then, and tucked the blanket back around me. "There now, lovely," she said. She patted my leg, and left.

I looked at Samuel, who was preparing to feed me. He lifted the spoon now.

"Come, now, little Ruth," he said, coaxing. "Open your mouth now."

I was not hungry. Knowing I'd been laid up in bed like this, my daughter apart from me, and Ma knowing about our engagement, angered me.

"No," I said staunchly. "I am not hungry, and I have much I need to discuss."

His eyes narrowed, but he lowered the spoon. "There are *many* things we need to discuss," he replied. "But what's most important at this juncture is you're doin' as you're told. So first, you open your mouth. You may be sick, but I'll keep a tally on disobedience, young lady."

Anger rose in me then, hot fury at all things that were unfair, the unsettled dreams I had, and the knowledge that for days, I'd been in bed and at the mercy of those around me. Ma knew we were betrothed. Did she know about the baby? And I wanted to see my daughter. But why had Samuel promised me a reckoning then? He'd already told me he wouldn't spank me when I was with child.

I felt a sharp pain in my abdomen. I clutched my sides, drawing my knees to my chest.

It was then that I knew. The whispered words. The flitting eyes. The regret that tinged Ma's words. I felt the telltale signs without having made the connection. The realization hit me like dousing torrent of icy rain, chilling me, lashing against my skin, and I fought to push the pain off my chest. It wouldn't budge.

I closed my eyes. The effort of keeping my eyes open was too much to bear. When I spoke to Samuel, my voice was a whisper, as I didn't trust myself to speak too loudly.

"There's no baby, is there?" I whispered. "I'm not with child."

My eyes still closed, I heard the clink of the bowl lowered to the table as Samuel shifted forward. I felt him lift my hand, and both his hands were around my one.

"No," he said softly. "I'm sorry, Ruth. You weren't sick from carryin' a child. Others have come down with the same illness you've had, and none were with child."

My eyes opened to look at his blue eyes, sympathetic and kind.

"There's no baby, honey."

I slumped against my pillows, the weight still pressed against my chest. I could feel the cramping. I felt the distance between me and Hannah, and I wanted to hold my little girl close. I felt my empty stomach and weakened limbs. I wanted to close my eyes and sleep, as I felt suddenly very, very empty. The effort to talk was too much. It was too much to sit up. I found inhaling deep breaths difficult, even, and opted instead to breathe in and out in slow, measured breaths.

I wanted to weep. I wanted to close my eyes and sleep.

I lifted a hand to my brow and draped my arm across my face. I wanted to block it out, everything, shut out the pain and the sadness and hurt.

I needed something, only I didn't know what it was I needed until he sat down on the bed, drawing me into his arms and holding me against his chest. I did not cry, though I wanted to. I allowed his strength and fortitude to seep through me. The hurt did not lift, but somehow, I was able to not be crushed beneath the weight of it all.

"I love you," he whispered. I could not reply. I nodded, accepting what he offered me, but unable to give him anything in return. We stayed like that a good long while, until I sat up straighter.

"Thank you," I whispered. "I'm stronger now. Thank you."

He released me and stood, picking up the now cold bowl of broth and sitting down next to me.

"Now, we've got to get some of this in your belly, honey," he said. "We need you better. You'll not refuse me, Ruth, and if you disobey me, I'll remember it." He was trying to be stern. I knew he was. But it was for my own good that he was being stern with me, and I didn't have the heart to disobey.

With a sigh, I gave in, opening my mouth and allowing him to spoon feed me some broth. I took one bite after another, not really hungry, and not really enjoying the taste, but as he fed me, he murmured things like, "that's my good girl," and "just one more bite now, honey." As he continued, I realized I yearned for just one more word of praise from him. Somehow, it satisfied a need in me, knowing he was proud of me.

Even if I couldn't bear him a child. Even if I couldn't keep a lid on my temper. Even if I was sick, and weak, and I obeyed him so sporadically.

Even if we were no longer to be wed.

There was no baby, as I'd suspected, but instead sickness. I closed my eyes against the sadness that rushed over me. Then it dawned on me that if Ma knew there was no baby, she'd clearly been privy to the fact that there might've been.

I closed my eyes and placed my head back on the pillow, as Samuel's large hand came to rest on my temple. He smoothed back the hair. "Talk to me, little Ruth," he said. I shook my head. I didn't even know where to begin. It all seemed hopeless, and so sad. My head swam. I felt suddenly warm again.

"I'm not leavin' you tonight," Samuel said. To some it would be a scandal, but I could not be terribly bothered with that knowledge. I was weak shortly after I finished the soup.

I no longer felt the nausea, or had a headache. Though I appreciated his gesture, I had to maintain some semblance of decorum.

"Samuel, I can't be bothered by what others think of me. I really and truly cannot," I insisted. "However, I'll not have you taint your good name by staying at the home of a widow. It's not right. You know it isn't. And I hate the idea of any of them talking about you. What if Hannah knows you're here again? I know Ma isn't going to say anything. But people in town, they'll talk."

"Let 'em talk," he growled. "And I'll be sure Hannah doesn't know I'm stayin' here. Don't forget, she'll be goin' to Ma's when she and Matthew return. She's been there for a few days now."

"You'll have chores to tend to at home!" I said.

"Geraldine, Phillip, and Matthew are handling the chores," Samuel said. "Everything's just fine at home. And I couldn't care less about what everyone in town says."

I wanted to kiss him and shake him all at once. I *hmphed* at him.

He narrowed his eyes. "Remember that tally, little lady. I'm not gonna lick you now when you're just gettin' over bein' sick and dealin' with the knowledge that… well, what you've just found out. But I will tan your pretty little backside when you're well again, you mark me."

I frowned, though I felt partly pleased with his attention. Still. Confound the man.

"There's nothing I can do to keep you from doing what you damn well please, now, is there?" I asked.

He reached over and tugged the loose braid that hung down by my ears. "Now you're up to a good twenty, sweetheart," he said.

I glared. "Why? I've just woken up a few minutes ago."

"It's pretty impressive how quickly you racked those licks up, truth be told," he said, with another tug.

I sighed heavily. I didn't find this amusing. I didn't find *anything* amusing. I closed my eyes. I heard him stand and place whatever he was holding down, then felt the bed shift beside me. I wanted him to hold me, and I wanted to push him away.

"C'mere, honey," he said softly. I opened my eyes. He was propped up next to me, and he opened his arms for me to come in. With a sigh, I nestled in, my head against his chest.

I knew now we were not getting married. The only reason for our betrothal was now gone. The loss of everything seemed so keen, I could hardly stand it. But I didn't want to say anything to him about it either, as I felt he'd be sure to protest. I didn't want to listen to the protests. I closed my eyes, still weak from the illness that'd ravaged me. I felt his hand smoothing my hair, starting at the top of my head and smoothing down until he got to my shoulders, then traveling back up again. I sighed, doing my very best to relax. For the second time, I fell fast asleep upon his chest.

• • • • • •

I woke in the middle of the night, more than once. Thunder clapped outside my window, lightning streaking across the night sky, I was still wearing naught but my chemise, and Samuel had changed. I could see the dishes had been cleared away, and the room was darkened but tidied. My clothes were neatly folded upon my chest, and Samuel's clothes lay next to mine. I wanted this to be our normal; his clothes next to mine, him next to me in bed. I didn't want him to go. He snored softly beside me, curled up on his side with his back to me. I rolled over on my side, my hand on my abdomen, as I felt another spasm of pain. I shifted, putting my arms around him, and closed my eyes. I would wake up, and when I did, everything would be okay.

• • • • • •

The next day, Samuel was up before I was, and when I

woke, he had a cup of milk and a plate of bread.

"Mornin', beautiful," he said. "How are you now?"

"I'm fine," I said shortly. I didn't want to get used to waking up next to him. It was easier not to. So I didn't want to talk. And I wanted to see my daughter. "May I get up after I've eaten?"

He nodded, eyes narrowed slightly, as he likely noticed the shift in my demeanor. I couldn't allow myself to be too vulnerable near him, not now. There was far too much at stake. I couldn't allow him to love me. Not when I had nothing to offer him. He needed a woman who was willing to submit to his highhanded ways, a young woman untarnished by her past, a woman who would offer him her innocence and purity. Not me. I had nothing to offer him.

"You eat your breakfast, and we'll see how you feel after that, young lady," he said sternly. I looked at him shyly. I did so like when he called me that. Still, I wouldn't cower.

"All right, then," I said. "Sounds acceptable. *Sir.*"

His eyes narrowed at me. "Tally," he warned.

I stuck my tongue out at him.

We both started when a knock came at the door.

He pointed a finger at the bed. "You stay put."

With a sigh, I obeyed. He handed me my breakfast, and I dutifully nibbled while he went to go answer the door.

I heard the low murmur of voices rising and falling, and as they continued, I began to grow concerned. The voices sounded upset. I needed to know what was going on, but if I got out of bed, I knew I'd eventually answer for my disobedience. Frowning, I waited, my impatience growing with each minute that passed. Fortunately, I didn't have to wait long. Moments after Samuel had left the room, he returned with Ma. Samuel looked grave, Ma nearly stricken. She was wringing her hands. The food grew heavy in my stomach.

"What's wrong?" I asked.

Ma looked to Samuel, who faced me. He cleared his throat. "Ma came here looking for Matthew and Hannah,

Ruth. She assumed when they didn't return last night that Hannah had come home to see you, and since I wasn't home, that I'd had Matthew stay here as well. But they're neither here nor at Ma's, and no one's seen them since they set out berry pickin' yesterday afternoon."

A chill crept over me. "What do you mean?" I asked, unable to fully comprehend what he was saying.

"No one knows where they are," he said. "But we'll find them."

I closed my eyes briefly. My little girl was lost. I could hardly bear it. Opening my eyes again, I turned to them. "Does anyone have any idea where they are? Anyone at all?"

Ma shook her head. "All's I know is that they were berry pickin'." She wrung her hands. "Oh, this is my fault. This is all my fault. I'm the one that sent them berry pickin' and I didn't tell anyone they didn't come back. I assumed they were here!"

I sighed as Samuel spoke up. "Ma, it ain't your fault. I stayed here last night to tend to Ruth, and that threw you off. If only I'd told you, we'd have known sooner they were missin'. You could put the blame on me as easily as anyone but sittin' around puttin' blame on anyone won't help. Now that we know they're missin', we've got to find them. Get Aaron and Phillip, and if we don't find 'em soon, we form a search party in town."

The hair on my arms stood on end. A search party. My stomach twisted in knots, but this time not from the nausea but fear.

"You have to let me look, Samuel," I said. Knowing that he'd put up a fuss, I put some gumption into my statement. He worked his jaw, and I knew he was debating what to do, make me stay or let me go against his better judgment.

"You're no help to us searchin' if you faint or go sick," Samuel said sternly. I knew he was right, but still, I had to find my girl. I simply had to.

"Then bring a wagon, and I'll sit on the wagon if need be," I said, swinging my legs over the side of the bed, suddenly realizing I was still wearing my chemise. I pulled the quilt up rapidly, but not before Ma'd caught a good look. My cheeks warmed.

She raised her brows and turned to her son but he merely shook his head. "You know I'm marryin' her," he said simply. I looked at him, my embarrassment at being caught dressed in only a chemise fading quickly. Would he still marry me, then? Hope rose in me.

"Best make it sooner than later's all I got to say on that," Ma replied. She winked at me as she left the room.

I rolled my eyes at Samuel. "Please leave so I can get changed," I beseeched him.

He merely crossed his arms. "*Tally.*"

I grunted, but ignored him as I rapidly changed. My head felt woozy at that point, and I did my very best to hide it so Samuel couldn't tell. I got to my feet unsteadily. Samuel came to my side and put my arm around his neck.

"Come with me," he said, and as we left my room, he whispered in my ear. "They likely just got lost somewhere nearby, and we'll find them real soon, honey. You try not to get yourself all worked up. It's gonna be all right, Ruth."

I nodded, remembering the dream I'd had with Hannah lost in the woods, and my frantic search for her. I couldn't bear to think of it now but simply had to push it out of my mind. The fear, however, had already settled in my stomach.

"We'll ride out to see Pearl and Aaron, Geraldine and Phillip. We'll have everyone in town searchin' for them if need be. The sooner we arrange a rescue party the better."

"Okay," I whispered. "We've got to find them, Samuel."

"We will, honey." He paused, reaching for my chin and lifting my eyes to his. "You are brave, Ruth. My brave, strong girl. We will find them, and you'll pull through this."

I nodded, but I wasn't so sure.

I'd lost so much already, lost so much in just the past few days, it was not unfathomable that even now I could lose what was more precious to me than my own life.

• • • • • •

We searched for hours. Samuel insisted I eat every once in a while, and I obeyed automatically, desperate to be allowed to stay in the search party for my little girl.

"Hannah!" I yelled, hearing the deeper echoes of Hannah and Matthew's names throughout the forest as Phillip, Aaron, and Samuel were all looking for both children. Geraldine stayed back at the wagon with her baby, in case someone had news for her, or by some chance she caught sight of Matthew or Hannah. I, however, was granted permission to traipse with Samuel deep into the woods, under the condition that I tell him if I felt sick. We first went to the berry bushes where they were supposed to have gone. They were picked clean, a sign that either the birds had already stripped them bare, or Hannah and Matthew had picked their fill before getting lost. But the children were nowhere to be found. Had they at least been here first? We couldn't tell. What had kept them from coming home to us?

I thought of the theft in town, the new men coming for a job upon the stagecoach, the new fur traders. It was more than I could bear, the thought of a criminal hurting my little girl. Stealing a saddle or someone's eggs was a far cry from harming a child, though. These were the things I told myself to ease my trepidation. Samuel said nothing about his fears, but merely searched without faltering. The longer time went on, as the sun ahead shone down, the more nervous I became.

"Matthew!" came Aaron's voice a good distance away.

"Where could they *be*?" I wailed.

"I don't know," Samuel muttered under his breath. "But when I catch that boy, I'm gonna wear him out good."

I knew it was only his fear talking, but I felt similar anger. How could they have gotten lost? The berry patch wasn't far from Ma's home at all, a mere stone's throw. What direction had they traveled? With each minute that passed, my nervousness grew. If they were missing for days, they risked dehydration, starvation, or worse. What would I do if my little girl was gone forever?

I squeezed my eyes, not willing to allow myself to even ponder the grim possibility. With my eyes closed, I suddenly remembered the night before, having woken in the dark, and the flash of lightning that lit up the night sky.

"The rain! The rain, Samuel!" I said, tugging on his sleeve excitedly.

He frowned at me. "Whatever are you talkin' about?" he said.

"It rained last night! They must've gotten caught in the rain. Maybe they got lost, and couldn't find their way home, then when the rain came they ran to get cover. We need to think of a place where they'd run to. Where would they run to for cover?"

He scratched his beard. "Well, there's the Tucker homestead beyond the hill," he said, extending a finger. "But I doubt they'd go that far." As he continued pushing past the branches of the trees, one snapped back and nearly struck him. He ducked just in time. But it reminded me of the day that I ran from Samuel when he was going to spank me. He'd gotten whacked across the face from the branches then, and what had I seen—something nearby that was a vague recollection. Somewhere they could've gone to, hidden from our vision by our house, but not far from our home, so close by that he actually had carried me over his shoulder all the way home once I'd let him. The cave.

"The cave!" I shouted. "They may have gone to the cave!"

"Cave?" Samuel asked, puzzled.

"It's not far from my cabin," I said. "Remember that day that you chased me and threw me over your shoulder, and took me back to the cabin?"

He scratched his chin.

"You forgot about throwing me over your shoulder?" I asked incredulously. Of all the things to forget! I could jog

151

his memory. "You, um… spanked me after."

His eyes lit up with recognition, and I rolled my eyes.

"That's right," he said. "Well, it's worth goin' to see if they're there," he said.

I couldn't remember exactly where it was, and I suddenly felt overcome with weakness. My knees wobbled, but I had to go. I *had* to get there. I ignored my weakened condition and plodded on, but Samuel was no fool.

"Ruth," he said warningly.

"It's nothing," I said. "*Please*, Samuel. Let me go. Please."

"No," he said staunchly. "You're going back to the wagon with Geraldine."

I yanked my arm from him, my frantic need to get to my little girl making me crazed. "Let me go!" I screamed as he took my arm firmly.

He shook his head. "Young lady, you are not goin' to pull this, or so help me, Ruth, I'll take you across my knee *now*."

A sob caught in my throat and I yanked away from him. Before I knew what was happening, he pulled me into him. His arms were around me. I struggled, but he held fast, so tightly I couldn't move. I tried to, but he held on until the fight went out of me.

"Listen, Ruth," he said, his voice hardening. "Woman, you *listen* to me."

I nodded.

"You're no help to your little girl if you faint along the way, now are you?"

I shook my head, unable to speak.

"I'm takin' you to the wagon. I'll drive. When you're strong enough to walk, I'll take you with me. We'll find them, Ruth. We will. They're out here, and we'll find them. We'll look at the cave. We'll form a bigger search party. Ma's already in town with the sheriff. That boy, we raised him right and he knows how to survive out here. He'll make sure your little girl's all right. And your little girl, she's got her mama's backbone, and she's a survivor. Trust me, honey.

You need to come with me now."

I had to believe him. I had to trust him. And I knew then, in that moment, when he held me in his arms, what I needed. For the first time, it all seemed to fall into place.

I needed someone strong, someone just that much stronger than I was, as Aaron had said, to tame the wild torrent within me. I needed stern. I needed uncompromising and rock solid. I needed someone who could handle my sass.

But it was hard to admit. It was hard to accept, until I had little choice. Run, or give in.

I would run no longer.

"All right," I said. "I'll trust you. Help me find my girl."

• • • • • • •

"Where is it, Samuel? Do you know?" I asked.

"Just up ahead," he said. "I remember exactly where it is. I know you were in no position to see where we were goin' at the time. But I know where it is."

I sniffed. Of course he did. Aaron, Phillip, and Geraldine had gone into town to join up with the search party. We were all to meet back at my home in an hour to see if anyone had any details. It only took a few minutes before we made it to where I remembered running from Samuel. I recognized the broken pine, with the limbs askew, only now the branches were drier and the needles a rusty orange. That was it. We were near.

"This! Here! Stop the wagon!" I shouted. Samuel drew up the reins.

I was just about to jump out, when I stopped. "May I get out? Please?" I asked him. It felt different asking permission like this. But I'd decided to trust him. He would lead.

"You may," he said solemnly. "But as we're walkin', if you feel faint, you'll come back to the wagon. Won't you? You remember the tally?"

I nodded. "Yes, sir."

His eyes warmed at that. He jumped down from the wagon ahead of me, reaching his hands to me. He grasped me about the waist and swung me down. I tried to walk quickly. If Hannah and Matthew had gotten lost by the cave, we would find them, and if not, maybe somebody back at the house had good news for us. I would stay calm. Samuel wanted me to stay calm.

As I walked in the direction where I knew the cave was, something bright yellow caught my eye.

Hannah's hair ribbon.

The hair on my arms stood on end as I raced ahead, plucking it from a cluster of ferns near the foot of a large oak.

"It's her hair ribbon," I gasped. "Oh, Samuel. It's Hannah's! I think we may be near them!" I turned back around. "Hannahhhh! Matthewww!" I shouted. Samuel's deeper voice joined in with mine, and as we shouted their names, we finally came to the mouth of the cave.

"This is it," I whispered. "Oh, Samuel, I hope my instinct is right, that they came here for shelter. Please, God."

I came up to the mouth of the cave and shouted. At first, I thought I heard something and my heart gave a great leap, but I realized quickly it was merely an echo. "Hannah! Matthew!"

Samuel walked ahead of me with the lantern. I followed. The second time I shouted, I heard something in return. Wide-eyed, I turned to Samuel. "Was that my imagination? Tell me it wasn't just in my mind."

He was already moving into the cave. "No, I heard it, too," he said.

He'd taken the lantern from the wagon Ma'd insisted we bring, and the light now shone brightly within the cave. We called their names again, and heard, louder this time, a resounding reply. My heart raced. They were here. We just had to find them. I felt myself growing woozy but I couldn't leave now, no matter if I'd promised him I would go. I had given my word, but we were just on the cusp of finding them. The lantern threw light into the inky darkness, and Samuel turned a corner, ducking low, as he held my hand tightly.

"Ma!"

I heard it louder now, Hannah's little voice. She was calling me. My girl was alive. We walked on and on, rounding bends and curves. It grew colder and darker, but the light of the lantern shone on.

"Hannah, where are you?" I shouted. My head grew light and I thought I'd faint, but I plowed on. And there, in the darkness, with nothing but the light of the lantern, I saw my little girl. She was crouched beside Matthew, who looked like he was asleep. I ran to her, dizzy with nausea and weakness, but stronger when I finally held Hannah. I knelt down beside Matthew, but Samuel had gotten there before me.

"What happened to him?" Samuel asked as I inspected Hannah. She appeared unharmed. His voice was laced with worry, though he kept calm.

"We were running out of the rain, Mr. Stanley. And there were these men, I don't know who or what they were about, but Matthew spied Aaron's saddle on one of their horses and he lit after them."

Samuel swore under his breath as Hannah continued. "They hit him across the head and someone knocked into his leg, and he fell over. They took off and he was madder than a hornet, but it was pouring by then, so we ran to the cave. That was last night, after dusk fell. He fell asleep, and has been mumbling in his sleep. Keeps telling me to stay safe and stay in the cave."

Samuel shook him gently. "Matthew?"

Matthew's eyes fluttered open. "Samuel," Matthew mumbled, trying to sit up. He put his hand to his head. "Ohh, my head. I think my leg's busted. Those confounded—" He suddenly noticed me and Hannah there, and he shook his head, biting his lip. "I found the lowlifes that took Aaron's saddle, and they hit me, then took off. Like as not they's the ones causin' all the trouble in town, but they're gone now. Hannah went lookin' for help but got caught in the rain again, and came back here and I tol' her to get back on in here cuz she didn't know where she was and was like as not to get lost alone in the forest. She left her hair ribbon out there, just about the only smart thought she had all day, because that girl—"

"That girl's my daughter that you've had in a cave all night, young man," I said sternly, raising a brow. He looked sheepish, and looked up at Samuel.

"I'm not so sure what I done wrong 'cept didn't come home last night. Couldn't find our way back, but I'm sure I got myself in trouble some way, didn't I?"

Samuel looked as relieved as I did. He still looked stern but his lips quirked. "I think this time you're lucky to be alive, boy," he said. "And we'll let you off the hook *this* time. But don't you go gettin' lost again, or I'll wear you out good. You hear?"

Matthew smiled sheepishly. "Yessir."

We walked together, ready to go home, as the sun peaked out of the clouds. My heart soared with joy and relief. I'd found my little girl. With Samuel holding one hand and Hannah the other, I walked toward the wagon, holding everything that was precious to me in my own two hands.

• • • • • • •

"Well, now, wigglin' that little backside's only gonna earn you more licks, little lady," Samuel said, but it was mock sternness this time, and none of the serious lecturing I'd gotten on previous sessions over his knee. It had been several days since we found Hannah and Matthew, and Samuel was now making good on his tally.

I wiggled my bottom even more. Since I was straddling one of his knees while lying over the bed, it served a dual purpose. I moaned out loud just before his hand connected to my bare skin.

Swat!

"Naughty little thing," he growled, but my punishment a second later was a finger thrust into my core, and I knew he wasn't really angry with me. It seemed Samuel had more than a spanking in mind.

"What happens to my girl if she disobeys?" Samuel asked. I could feel his hand poised over my vulnerable bottom.

"She gets a spanking," I moaned, in a voice thick with desire.

"That's right, honey," he said softly, another sharp swat landing, stoking my desire for him. His fingers probed my sex as I writhed against him, reveling in his power and strength.

He spanked me harder, each stroke making my need for him grow, until I was on the edge of losing all control.

"Pretty little, naughty little girl," he whispered, his hand smoothing over my warmed skin just before it rose and fell again. The sound of the spank echoed in the room, mingling with my moans and his heavy breathing. I felt his hands about my waist, lifting me up, placing me on my back. I opened my arms, welcoming him to come closer to me. As he lowered his body down upon mine, I knew then that I'd surrendered, not just my body, not just my will. No more did I doubt he loved me. I was wanted, I was cherished, and I was loved.

EPILOGUE

The sun shone on the day Hannah released the little birds from her room. It was fitting to see their little wings unfold and fly, as they soared away, her eyes filled with tears. They'd come to us when we were as broken as they, and now they were set free. Now they'd grown stronger. Now they would fly.

She tied the bow on the back of the lovely dress I'd borrowed from Geraldine for my wedding. I didn't know it would fit, but it did. It was an ivory silk, the likes of which I'd never laid eyes on, much less worn. But it seemed fitting I'd wear a dress befitting a queen on the day I would say "I do" to my Samuel.

Hannah helped me into the matching kid slippers, while Pearl affixed the white roses in my hair. I stood, looking at my reflection in the mirror. I hardly recognized myself. My eyes shone brightly, my cheeks full and flushed, my dark hair gleaming in the sunlight that streamed through the window.

"Oh, you're pretty as a picture," Ma whispered as she kissed my cheek. She tucked a stray hair behind my ear, and smoothed an imaginary wrinkle from my skirt. "Just lovely. Samuel is fit to be tied waitin' for you, darlin'. Let's get you to your groom."

My groom.

I walked out to him gingerly, lest the flowers fall from my hair or I'd wake and find it was all a dream. I followed my pretty little girl, bedecked in a new dress of her own, as she tossed rose petals on the floor in front of me. Ma's cabin was barely recognizable, it had been adorned in so many flowers. It was a simple affair, Samuel's family—*our* family—standing by, holding flowers and babies while I walked to my future husband. Samuel was handsome in his Sunday best, and as he reached for my hand, he drew me close.

"You're too pretty to be seen in public," he whispered.

"Well, now, isn't that romantic," I quipped.

He kissed my cheek and whispered in my ear. "Addin' that to the tally, little Ruth. It means a lot more once you're my wife." His eyes danced. Though he'd already made good on that tally, it seemed he'd be starting up another, but I didn't care a lick.

I laughed with abandon and joy as I whispered, "I love you."

He leaned into my ear and whispered one final time to me before we took our vows. "I love you, little Ruth, and I'm pleased to make you mine."

THE END

STORMY NIGHT PUBLICATIONS WOULD LIKE TO THANK YOU FOR YOUR INTEREST IN OUR BOOKS.

If you liked this book (or even if you didn't), we would really appreciate you leaving a review on the site where you purchased it. Reviews provide useful feedback for us and for our authors, and this feedback (both positive comments and constructive criticism) allows us to work even harder to make sure we provide the content our customers want to read.

If you would like to check out more books from Stormy Night Publications, if you want to learn more about our company, or if you would like to join our mailing list, please visit our website at:

www.stormynightpublications.com

Made in the USA
Middletown, DE
28 February 2019